"Tristan?"

He glanced over at her. "Yes?"

Her gaze immediately latched on to his lips. They were full, nice, inviting. She felt a sudden pull in her stomach. She wondered how they would feel if she were to press hers against them.

"Dani?"

She snatched her gaze from his lips up to his eyes. They were eyes that were studying her intently. "What?"

"You called my name. What did you want?"

Frowning, Danielle compressed her lips, deciding for the moment to keep her mouth closed or else she might say the wrong thing. There was no way she would tell him that for a crazy moment she had been ready to ask if she could sample his lips.

"Dani? What's wrong?"

If only he knew.

Books by Brenda Jackson

Kimani Romance

Solid Soul
Night Heat
Risky Pleasures
In Bed with Her Boss
Irresistible Forces
Just Deserts

Kimani Arabesque

Tonight &Forever
A Valentine Kiss
"Cupids Bow"
Whispered Promises
Eternally Yours
One Special Moment
Fire and Desire
Something to Celebrate
"Truly Everlasting"
Secret Love
True Love
Surrender

Silhouette Desire

*Delaney's Desert Sheikh
*A Little Dare
*Thorn's Challenge
Scandal Between the Sheets
*Stone Cold Surrender
*Riding the Storm
*Jared's Counterfeit Fiancée
Strictly Confidential Attraction
Taking Care of Business
*The Chase Is On
*The Durango Affair
*Ian's Ultimate Gamble
*Seduction, Westmoreland Style
**Stranded with the Tempting Stranger
*Spencer's Forbidden Passion
*Taming Clint Westmoreland
*Cole's Red-Hot Pursuit

*Westmoreland family titles
**The Garrisons

BRENDA JACKSON

is a die "heart" romantic who married her childhood
sweetheart and still proudly wears the "going steady" ring he
gave her when she was fifteen. Because she's always believed
in the power of love, Brenda's stories always have happy
endings. In her real-life love story, Brenda and her husband
of thirty-six years live in Jacksonville, Florida, and have two
sons.

A *USA TODAY* bestselling author of more than fifty romance
novels, Brenda is also a recent retiree who worked thirty-
seven years in management at a major insurance company.
She divides her time between family, writing and traveling.
You may write to Brenda at P.O Box 28267, Jacksonville,
Florida 32226; e-mail her at WriterBJackson@aol.com or
visit her Web site at www.brendajackson.net.

BRENDA JACKSON

JUST DESERTS

KIMANI™
ROMANCE

KIMANI PRESS™

ISBN-13: 978-0-373-86072-2
ISBN-10:   0-373-86072-2

JUST DESERTS

www.kimanipress.com

Printed in U.S.A.

Dear Reader,

It was a great pleasure to work on a project with two good author buddies of mine, Carla Fredd and Carmen Green!

From the moment we decided to write this trilogy, I was fascinated with Danielle's character. I knew she would be a likable person, but she would also be someone who was hurting from the deceit of a man she thought was her husband.

And then there was Tristan, her best friend and, unbeknownst to Danielle, the man who has secretly been in love with her for years. I found myself rooting for Tristan and hoping that Danielle would finally realize what was right before her eyes.

I took the following question to my book club: "Can you fall in love with your best friend?" The responses were great and thought-provoking and started a lot of discussions. Overwhelmingly, we agreed that starting out as best friends makes for the best relationships.

I hope all of you enjoy reading Tristan and Danielle's story, where you will see if that holds true.

Also, I would love for you to join me for the Madaris Family Reunion Cruise to Canada out of New York in June 2009. Please visit my Web site for more details!

Happy reading!

Brenda Jackson

Acknowledgment

To the love of my life, Gerald Jackson, Sr.
Happy 36th anniversary!

To my author buddies, Carla Fredd and Carmen Green.
I had fun working with you ladies on this one.
Let's do it again!

To everyone who will be joining me on the 2009
Cruise to Canada. This one is for you!

For if a man think himself to be something,
when he is nothing, he deceiveth himself.
—*Galatians* 6:3

Chapter 1

If it had been left up to Tristan Adams, he would not have given Danielle Timmons-Foster the news. But it hadn't been left up to him. For the past two months her life had been one hellacious lie. A part of him wondered if one more lie wouldn't hurt. But for Danielle he knew it would.

And when she hurt, he hurt.

She had dropped onto the sofa and was staring at him as if he had totally lost his mind. He almost wished he had. Or, at least, that this episode had been one long nightmare they would finally wake up from—and find that not only was her husband not dead, but that he hadn't left three wives behind. Three wives who, until a couple of months ago, each assumed they were Mrs. Marc Foster. And now to add salt to the wound, he'd just told Danielle there might be a fourth woman out there with the title, as well.

"Tristan, please tell me you're joking," Danielle said, her voice soft, low and sounding utterly defeated. "It's a sick joke, but I'll accept it. I don't want to believe what you just said. I *can't* believe what you just said."

He nodded slowly, understanding. He had been with her when she'd gotten the call two months ago that her husband of five years was dead after having choked on—of all things— his wedding ring. He'd also been with her at Marc's funeral in California when they'd discovered she wasn't the only Mrs. Foster. And he'd been by her side at the attorney's office when it had been declared that the second wife, Renée, was the legal Mrs. Foster and that Danielle, his first wife, and Alexandra, his third, had gotten duped with phony marriage licenses.

He released a long sigh and crossed the living room's hardwood floor to sit beside Danielle on the sofa. He took her hand in his and tried to smile. "Dani, I stopped teasing you the day you began wearing your first training bra, remember?"

He knew that would get a smile out of her. She would remember that day. It would remind her of happier times when her brother had been alive. Tristan couldn't help but smile himself whenever he thought of Paul Timmons, his best friend since kindergarten. They'd lived in the same neighborhood and had gone to school together, had played peewee football and gone off to college together—roommates at the University of Florida in Gainesville, a long way from their hometown of Port St. Lucie, Florida. And then when they'd finished college, they'd returned home to go into business together. They started A&T Shipping Company, making it into a very successful corporation. Then the Iraq war started and Paul's reserve unit was shipped out for duty. Paul never made it back home alive.

"When will it end?" Danielle asked, her words intruding into his thoughts. "How could I have been married to a man and not know him the way I thought I did?"

Tristan's grip on her hand tightened. They had covered this ground before and he felt partly to blame. Danielle had been a well-known international model when she had been contacted about Paul's death. Since their parents had gotten killed in a plane crash her first year in college, Paul had been all the family she'd had. Losing him had taken a toll on her. Claiming she was tired of the glitz and glamour of life as a successful fashion model, she had returned to Port St. Lucie to take over Paul's role as Tristan's partner.

Barely two months after Paul's death, Marc Foster had opened a business account, and since Danielle's role was to wine and dine new clients, she had taken on Marc. If Tristan hadn't been so torn up with grief himself over losing his best friend, he would have seen Marc for the conniving snake he was. Marc had set his sights on Danielle and less than a month later, Danielle had called to say she and Marc had eloped to Atlanta.

The reason Tristan blamed himself was that he had promised Paul the day he'd left for Iraq that if anything were to happen to Paul, he would look after Danielle. Apparently he'd done a piss-poor job of it.

Danielle pulled her hand from his, stood up and began pacing the floor. It wasn't hard to realize she was madder than hell. He would be, too, if he were in her shoes.

She had dropped by last night for dinner and he had talked her into spending the night, since the guest room practically had her name on it, anyway. He knew she thought of him as nothing more than her best friend and confidant. He was hoping that one day she would begin to see him as more.

He leaned back in the sofa trying to recall when he had finally broken down and admitted to himself that he was in love with her. Had it been that day she'd called to say she'd eloped? That was probably the reason he had taken off a couple of days and drank himself into a stupor.

He had called himself all kinds of fool for letting Marc into her life, but not once had Tristan gotten out of line or tried convincing her to divorce the guy. He'd respected her marriage. He'd even tried to like Marc. When he saw that he couldn't, he'd gone five years and pretended he did.

But he should have suspected something wasn't on the up-and-up with the guy. Because Danielle confided in Tristan, he knew about the spats the couple had about Marc's job as a salesman and the frequency of his out-of-town trips. He also knew that they were on bad terms around the issue of children—Danielle wanted a child but Marc never seemed to have the time to slow down and give her one. Now they knew why. The man had been living a double life. Tristan took that back. Marc Foster had been living a *triple* life. And now, according to Marc's brother, Chris, who'd called late last night, there may have been a fourth woman involved.

"Who told you about the fourth woman?"

He glanced over at Danielle. She stood—all five foot eight of her—in a stance he found totally sexy. She was an absolutely gorgeous woman whose face and body had once graced the covers of a number of magazines. Her face was tilted at a haughty angle, her hands were on her hips, her feet were bare, and she was wearing a short skirt with an even shorter ribbed top. Today she looked more like twenty than thirty, with a body that made men weep.

His gaze zeroed in on her face. She had coffee-colored skin, dark almond eyes and lush, full lips. Her shoulder-length hair was tousled and sexy. She looked like she'd just crawled out of bed. Too bad it hadn't been his.

Dani didn't know how he felt about her. Didn't have a clue. She assumed their relationship—as it had always been—was that of little sister and big brother. Boy, was she wrong. At thirty-four, he could no longer think of her as a little sister. She was a full-grown woman in every sense of the word. But he would continue to be her best friend until she finally opened her eyes to see just how things really were.

"Tristan?"

Her saying his name reminded him that he hadn't answered her question. "Chris called after you went to bed last night."

She inhaled and he watched the movement of her chest when she did so. The low cut of her top displayed the top swell of her breasts. "Do Alex and Renée know?"

He shrugged. "Yes. Chris mentioned he told Renée and that he had spoken to Hunter to relay the news to Alexandra."

He thought about the three women, who at Marc's funeral had quickly become bitter enemies. Over the past couple of months, however, after discovering that Marc had been a pathological liar, they had actually bonded. Marc had betrayed all three of them. And now there might be a fourth one out there.

Alexandra and Hunter Smith had gotten

married last month, and Renée and Chris Foster were engaged and would be getting married later this month. Hunter was Chris's friend. He'd agreed to fly to Atlanta and escort Alexandra to Marc's funeral in California two months ago.

"How did Chris find out?"

Tristan hesitated before saying anything, deciding to give her the skimmed-down version without a lot of detail. If he told her everything, she'd be more upset. "It seems that Marc had a locker at the airport. Chris had all Marc's mail at that post-office box in Costa Woods forwarded to him, and two days ago he received a renewal notice for the locker. Chris caught a plane out to California to check out the locker and found an apartment key inside it. After a little investigating he determined where the apartment was located and went there."

"And?"

"And from what he discovered, he reached the conclusion that there could be a fourth Mrs. Foster, or that Marc was planning another wedding. Chris leans toward the latter."

"The bastard!"

Tristan went to her and pulled her into his arms, wanting her to get her emotions out. She had cried in the attorney's office when it was revealed that Marc was sterile, but he felt she was still holding a lot inside. She refused to let all of it out.

She pulled away from his arms. "No, I won't cry again," she said angrily. "If I cry again that means Marc has succeeded in humiliating me again. And I won't let him."

Danielle walked back over to the sofa and calmly sat down. "Now, Tristan," she said in a composed voice, "does Chris know how to contact the woman?"

He sat beside her. "No," he said.

"Who's been paying the rent?"

"Chris spoke with the landlord and it appears Marc had a paid-up lease for a full year."

Danielle nodded. "And from what Chris found at the apartment he's pretty sure there might be a fourth woman?"

"Yes, it's a very good possibility."

She stood up again. "Then we have to do

something. We need to find out if she was a wife or a fiancée. We need to—"

He pulled her back down on the sofa beside him. "*We*, namely *you*, need to slow down and relax, Danielle. You've been through a lot these past two months and I don't want to see you lose it."

She lifted a brow. "Lose it?"

"Yes. Have a nervous breakdown or something," he tried to say delicately. "I don't want to see you lose control."

She scoffed at his words. "Oh, come on, Tris. I'm always in control. I'm—"

"Danielle," he said in a firm voice, "do I need to remind you that you lost it one day and slapped someone? You, who're too compassionate to even squish a bug, actually slapped Alexandra."

He watched as she lowered her head in shame. Then she raised her head and he noted first regret and then fire in her eyes. "Okay, that was one time I admit I lost it. Hell, Tristan, she pissed me off. If you had any idea what she said—"

"I know what she said. She told us and she apologized."

"And I apologized, as well. I even offered to let her slap me back," she said in earnest.

Tristan couldn't help but chuckle at the ridiculousness of the offer Danielle had made that day. "Well, still, you've been under a lot of emotional stress and pressure and need to get away."

"Get away?" she asked with an incredulous look on her face.

"Yes, get away."

"Tristan, I can't get away. I've taken enough time away from A&T as it is, trying to straighten out the mess Marc left me in."

"You can and you will. Take off, Danielle. Fly to New York and visit some of your friends. Or better yet, fly to Paris to visit that model friend of yours. What's her name?"

"Lust."

"On second thought maybe you don't need to fly to Paris."

A smile touched Danielle's face. "Trying to be big brother, Tristan?"

"Someone has to keep you out of trouble."

"Whatever."

"Now where were we? Oh, yeah, we were discussing your need to get away. And I don't want to hear any argument out of you."

She looked at him and he knew she was itching to make a word of protest, but she had to know it wouldn't do any good. When he had his mind made up, that was it. "Okay, okay. And if I do get away for a few days, when I come back will you promise to help me find out more about that fourth woman?"

He shook his head. "Dani, I'm sure Chris is already on it. He's an FBI agent, so he'll know how to track her down."

"Yes, but I want to be there when he does. You know how it was with Alex, Renée and me. One of us needs to be there to assure this woman that everything will be okay and that we were all duped by Marc and survived. Since I'm the oldest among Marc's wives, that task belongs to me."

Tristan studied her stubborn features, especially the firm set of her lips. They were lips he had placed a friendly kiss on a number of times but had never taken with the fire and passion that burned in his loins whenever he looked at them. "Okay, Danielle, I don't think Chris will have a problem with that. I'll run it by him the next time we talk."

"Thanks. And I also want to thank you for standing by me the way you have the past couple of months. You took time away from the company to be with me and I really appreciate it."

"Don't mention it."

"No, I feel I need to mention it, Tris. You've been super and you're the best friend a girl could have." She then leaned down and kissed his cheek before prancing off toward the guest room and closing the door behind her.

The moment Danielle closed the door behind her she grabbed her cell phone off the dresser. It was still early morning, but she hoped that Alex and Renée were out of bed already. And if they weren't that was too bad, because they needed to discuss this latest development.

She shook her head when she thought about

their relationship. At first it had been fiery, with each of them thinking she was the real Mrs. Foster and the other two were frauds. Tempers had flared, nasty words had been spoken, as Tristan had reminded her, she had even gotten physical. All because Marc had turned out to be a no-good bastard with a capital *B*. He had played each of them and played them well. He had taken over a million dollars from Alex and had even purchased a yacht Alex hadn't known he had. From Renée, he had taken her aunt Gert's priceless diamond necklace; luckily it had been recovered. As for herself, Marc had destroyed the one thing she wanted most from her marriage—a child.

When she, Alex and Renée had finally transferred their anger for each other to where it truly belonged—on Marc—they were able to sort things and see just how deep his deceit had gone. And now, according to Tristan, it may have gone deeper than any of them could have ever imagined.

"Hello."

"Alex, wake up. It's Danielle."

There was a pause and then. "Danielle, why are you calling at nine in the morning?"

She wanted to remind her that most people were out of bed by that time. Instead, she said, "Sorry, but we need to talk. Hold tight while I get Renée on the line."

Danielle shook her head and smiled as she punched in Renée's phone number. Alexandra, at twenty-one, was the youngest of the three, and when Danielle had first met her at Marc's funeral, Alex had come across as one ditzy chick with too much money on her hands, thanks to her wealthy family. What woman would show up at her dead husband's funeral wearing, of all things, a sleeveless white dress with black polka dots and some outlandish hat on her head? But after getting to know Alex, Danielle had discovered that she was actually quite smart.

But no one, Danielle decided, was smarter than Renée, wife number two, who at twenty-four was a college professor. Since the first grade Renée had attended exclusive boarding schools on academic scholarships, and people always considered her somewhat of a genius.

According to Renée, all she ever wanted to do was live a normal life, and she'd fallen for Marc because he was able to make her feel less like a brain and more like a woman.

"Yes?"

"Renée?" She sounded sleepy, too. Did everybody sleep late on Saturday morning? She wondered. "This is Danielle. I have Alex on the line. We need to talk. Hold on for a sec while I get her."

She then switched over to bring Alex on the line, only to discover she wasn't there, although she could hear noise in the background. "Alex? Are you there? What's going on?"

"Sorry about that, Danielle, but both Hunter and Little Sweetie don't like it that you woke them up."

Danielle rolled her eyes. Hunter was Alex's husband of less than a month, and Little Sweetie was Alex's dog, which Alex treated like a human being. "Apologize to them both, please, but by now I'm sure you've heard that there's a possibility Marc might have been engaged to another woman."

"Yes, we heard," Renée said. "And as far as I'm concerned, she should be counting her blessings that a wedding never took place."

"You're right," Danielle said. "But think of the emotional trauma it might cause her when she finds out about us."

"Maybe she won't find out," Alex said quietly. And then in a playful voice she said, "Stop that, Hunter. We can't mess around now. I'm talking to my wives-in-law."

Danielle rolled her eyes again at the term Alex had adopted to define their relationship. "What do you think we should do, Renée?" Danielle asked. At least she was certain she had Renée's attention. When a few seconds ticked by and Renée didn't respond, Danielle asked again. "Renée?"

"Oh, sorry. What was your question?"

Danielle wanted to throw the phone down and scream. There could be only one reason Renée was not focused. "Is Chris there with you, Renée?"

"Of course he's here. He lives here. Don't you remember I told you that he transferred to

Birmingham and is working for an agency here while we plan the wedding?"

"Sorry, I did forget. And how are the wedding plans coming along?"

"Fine. Just three more weeks to go. I'm getting excited."

Danielle couldn't help but be excited for her. Marc had been an ass and as far as she was concerned, both Alex and Renée deserved real happiness in their lives.

So did she.

But there was no way she could be happy until she uncovered the mystery surrounding the fourth woman. "Look, evidently this is not a good time to discuss anything with you two, so how about calling me back later? And Renée, it would be nice if Chris was included in our call. Then he could cover everything with us that he found at Marc's apartment."

"And what are you planning to do after that?" Alex asked on a yawn.

"I plan to find her."

"Take Tristan with you when you go looking for her," Renée said.

Danielle lifted a brow. "Why?"

"It will be fun," Renée answered.

"Besides, he seems to like spending time with you," Alex added.

Danielle knew what Alex and Renée were getting at. She was well aware that they thought something was going on between her and Tristan because of the time he had playfully kissed her hand in front of them. She had tried convincing them that she and Tristan were nothing more than best buddies, but evidently they didn't believe her. "Thanks for the suggestion, Alex. I just might do that. Goodbye."

Then she quickly hung up the phone.

An hour or so later, bored with the book she'd been reading, Danielle left the confines of her bedroom to look for Tristan. Funny how she considered the guest room at Tristan's house as *her* room. When had that started? She wondered. Right after Paul had died and she had left the modeling world to return to Port St. Lucie.

It was hard to convince the people she'd

known all her life that she was no longer Dani, the highly paid fashion model who'd walked numerous runways and been named one of the top models in the world by *People*.

And then when half the modeling world, including Tyra, Viva and Heidi, had shown up at Paul's funeral, her home—the one she and Paul had inherited after their parents' death—had become an overnight sensation, drawing thousands of people who drove by hoping to see a celebrity. So it had been Tristan's home where she would escape to whenever she needed to get away and find solace and peace.

Even after she'd married Marc and they had their little spats, it wasn't unusual for her to show up here late at night. And since she had her own key, sometimes Tristan wouldn't even know she was there until he awoke the next morning.

She smiled, remembering the time he had brought a date home only to find Danielle coming from the kitchen wearing a bathrobe. He'd had a lot of explaining to do, trying to convince Sharon What's-her-name that their relationship was strictly platonic.

Danielle rounded the corner and came to a stop. Tristan was stretched out on the sofa sound asleep. *Poor baby.* She tiptoed quietly over to him, understanding why he was so exhausted. Now that their business had expanded, grown by leaps and bounds, the two of them no longer had to be tied to the office to run things. Tristan, however, was still very much hands-on. Danielle loved her role working in PR and being all over the place. All the contacts she'd made over the years proved to be an asset in bringing new accounts A&T's way.

Stooping down, she studied Tristan's features, seeing how they'd changed over the years. He no longer had that boyish look. He had grown into an extremely handsome man. He had chocolate-colored skin and the most gorgeous dark eyes and lips she had ever seen on a man. His long eyelashes were to die for, but then, she couldn't discount his blunt nose and chiseled jaw. Both added arrogance to his features, a characteristic Tristan could not claim. He had to be the most humble man she knew.

His skin looked soft to the touch, and she

knew from experience it was. She fought back the temptation to touch him now. She remembered the crush she'd had on him at twelve, until that day she'd seen him kissing Sadie McClelland in the park. It had broken her heart. She had run home crying to her mother, who'd hugged her and explained that it wasn't real love she felt for Tristan but hero worship, and there was a big difference.

What her mother said that day had made real good sense at the time, but now Danielle couldn't help wondering if at one time during her life she had actually loved Tristan. Really loved him.

She almost gasped when his eyes flickered open and she suddenly felt trapped by his dark gaze. Something stirred within her that almost made her moan. She actually felt herself swaying. Inhaling deeply, she tried thinking of something to say, but he beat her to it.

"You were staring at me."

"Yes," she answered with a guilty nod. "You were sleeping and I didn't want to wake you."

He held her gaze a little longer and then

shifted positions to sit up. He rubbed his hands down his face. "Okay, I'm awake now, Dani. What's wrong?"

Dani.

That had always been his name for her, although Paul and her parents had stuck to Danielle. When she became a model it had been so easy to use the name he'd given her.

"Nothing's wrong. I just talked to Alex and Renée a few minutes ago."

"And?"

Danielle dropped down beside him, forcing him to scoot over to make room. "And neither of them seems interested in finding the fourth woman."

He took her hand in his, something he'd been doing a lot lately. "Dani, I think they're interested. They just don't have the fire about it that you do. I hate to tell you this, but now they have *lives*. Alexandra is married and Renée will be getting married this month. They have moved beyond what Marc did to them."

"And you don't think I have?"

He paused, as if choosing his words carefully. "I just don't think it's as easy for you to let go. Maybe it's because you were Marc's first wife. Or it could be because you were married to him the longest. But then, it might be your age."

Tristan swallowed, realizing he'd just made a mistake when he saw the narrowing of Danielle's eyes and the stiffening of her spine. "What about my age, Tris?"

Looking into her scowling face, he knew he had to smooth things over or get a cold shoulder the rest of the day. "What I mean, Dani, is that you're a lot more mature than Alexandra and Renée. That's not a bad thing. You've been where they have yet to go. What they are experiencing now is—"

"Men!"

He lifted a brow. "Excuse me?"

"Men," she said, as if with distaste. "Alex and Renée have a man in their lives. I'm not involved with anyone so I have a lot more personal time on my hands."

Tristan took a minute to fully absorb what she had said. "And why do you think that is,

Dani? Other than Marc, I've never known you to become involved with anyone, at least not seriously."

"Yeah, and look where my involvement with Marc got me. The man was a con artist extraordinaire. He caught me at a vulnerable time and swept me off my feet. The next thing I knew I was in Atlanta getting married."

"Because you thought you loved him?" he asked quietly, wondering what her answer would be. During the past five years there were times he actually thought she loved Marc, and then there were times he'd been filled with doubt.

She seemed to think deeply about his question and then she said, "No, because at that time I thought he loved me. I wanted someone to love me. I was hurt. I felt alone. And then Marc appeared and seemed capable of making me feel whole. Not special but whole. There is a difference."

He leaned back on the sofa. "And what's the difference?"

She leaned back with him. "I felt special

as a model. I was used to getting all kinds of attention, even when I didn't want it. But Marc made me see the importance of moving on after losing Paul, and he was there to help me get beyond my grief."

Tristan didn't say anything for a while. Marc had done for her what *he* should have done. He, Tristan, had let her down and in the interim left the door wide open for another man to walk in and have her. A part of him would never forgive himself for doing that. For five years he had to endure the pain of knowing the woman he loved had married someone else.

"Why did you stay with him if you didn't love him?" he finally asked.

She curled up by his side. He knew that to her it was a natural thing to do, no big deal. She had no way of knowing how her closeness was making his heart leap in his chest. "You of all people know how things were between me and Marc, Tris. I confided to you about it. We hadn't been married a year when I noticed he was taking more and more trips out of town and was becoming distant. There were blocks of time—and I mean huge blocks—when we didn't even share a bed when he was home. And when he was away he seldom called, claiming his business was keeping him extremely busy."

She paused for a moment, then continued, "I never told you this part, but I even threatened him with a divorce if he didn't get his act together. I was beginning to feel like we were married in name only. Hell, I was spending more time over here with you than at my house, because he was never there. When Hurricane Frances swept through here a few years ago, I was stranded with you the entire time while Marc was somewhere else."

Tristan nodded, remembering the time. They had been stuck here without any electrical power while her husband had been no telling where and with whom.

"You said you had threatened him with divorce. What happened to make you change your mind?"

She met his gaze. "A baby," she said softly. "He promised me a baby."

Tristan didn't say anything. All he could do was remember the day she found out that the one thing Marc had promised her had been the one thing he couldn't deliver. A case of the mumps in his teens had left him incapable of fathering a child. She had taken the news hard.

She turned to Tristan now, took hold of his hand as he had done hers so many times when they talked. She met his gaze. "You know how much I wanted a child. The last time Marc and I were together, I mean really together, was around eight months before he died. That night Marc promised that he would slow down his travels and take time to start the family he knew I wanted."

He felt her tighten her hold on his hand, and he squeezed back. "And you know what hurts, Tris? What really hurts?"

"No, what really hurts, Dani?"

He met her gaze and wished he hadn't. There were tears there, big tears, and he felt his heart stop. He wanted nothing more than to pull her into his arms, hold her and whisper how much he loved her and tell her that from now on he would not let anything or anyone hurt her again. But at this moment, she didn't need to hear what he had to say. She needed for him to listen.

"What really hurts, Tris, is knowing Marc never intended to keep that promise. He lied about that like he'd lied about so many other things."

And then she broke down and began crying in earnest, and he reached out and pulled her into his arms. He held her and told her not to cry, that things would work out fine, and that one day she would get the baby she wanted. The family she desired.

An inner part of Tristan broke, as well. The tears Danielle had refused to shed earlier were pouring like torrential rain. He could actually feel her pain.

And he knew at that moment that he would be the one to fulfill the promise Marc had broken, the one her dead husband had never intended to keep, the one that kept tearing her up inside. He would become her husband one day and give her the love and respect she deserved. He would cherish her, protect her.

She didn't know it yet, but one day she would.

Chapter 2

Danielle glanced over at Tristan. She knew at this point it would be a complete waste of her time to try to convince him she didn't need to get away, since they were on the plane, buckled in and waiting for takeoff. The only good thing was that he was coming with her and had agreed that on their way back from San Francisco they would make a stop in Alabama to attend Chris and Renée's wedding.

She had to admit she was excited about

going to San Francisco. She had spent a month in the Bay Area a few years back while doing a photo shoot, and looked forward to going just for fun and relaxation.

She watched Tristan key something into his BlackBerry. She hadn't wanted him to bring anything work related, but…that was the one concession she had ultimately agreed to when he had taken her up on her offer to come along: that he be allowed to check on things in the office periodically.

"How are things on the home front?" she decided to ask.

He looked up at her and smiled and not for the first time lately, his smile seemed to reach out and touch her in a way it hadn't before. She found the sensation odd, but was determined not to make a big deal out of it.

"Everything is fine. We should feel good that we have such a great work crew."

She knew that was true, but there was one thing she felt she needed to say. "Yes, but I see that Karin Stokes likes spending a lot of time in your office." She could tell by the look that suddenly appeared in his eyes that her obser-vation surprised him.

"Don't you think that's rather comical for you to say since she's my administrative assistant?"

She gave him a pointed look. "She's also a woman trying to hit on her boss. Trust me, I know. When is Madeline returning from her foot surgery, anyway?"

A part of Tristan wondered if Dani knew she was sounding like a jealous woman. He found it interesting. A slow, easy smile curved his lips when he said, "Madeline will be back in the office by the time we return."

He looked deep into her eyes. "Does that make you happy?" The same part of him dared her to deny it.

She didn't. "Yes, it makes me happy."

And as if that was that, she lay her head back and closed her eyes. Tristan couldn't stop the chuckle that formed deep in his throat. He wanted to ask her to explain herself, but halted the impulse. Why had she gotten possessive all of a sudden? Not that he was complaining. Still, he couldn't help but be curious.

Feeling rather smug, he put his head back and closed his eyes, too, remembering the past week. She'd spent the whole week in his guest room and hadn't returned home. He hadn't asked when she was leaving and she hadn't volunteered any information. They simply lived under the same roof in harmony as if it was nothing unusual for him to wake up each morning and find her there and to say goodnight to her when he turned in for bed.

He figured it was something about spending so much time at her house—the one she'd shared with Marc—that bothered her, and he was more than satisfied with going to bed at night knowing she was down the hall.

It had been downright difficult to get her to take a trip, but finally he'd managed to work out a deal with her. She was hell-bent on finding this fourth woman, so he had agreed to help her do so if she would get away for a while. So now here they were on a plane in the middle of the week, flying to San Francisco for a few days. He had even tried to get her to agree to a full week, but she had refused, saying that she wouldn't be able to rest until she found the fourth woman.

Chris had a few leads but had agreed not to do anything until they met with him. As Tristan had explained to Marc's brother, there was something driving Danielle to be the one to bring closure to what had happened. Somehow he knew it would only be then that she got some kind of emotional relief.

Danielle slowly opened her eyes, tilted her head and looked over at Tristan. His eyes were closed. She wondered what he was thinking about. Was he beginning to think she was a pain in the behind? Was he wondering when she would finally pack up her stuff and leave his house?

She knew she probably should do so soon, but the thought of going home dampened her already low spirits. She couldn't deal with the anger she felt each and every time she thought about Marc and all the things he'd done.

Deciding to read a book, she reached into her carry-on to grab the mystery novel she had started yesterday.

"You okay?" Tristan asked.

She glanced over at him again. His dark eyes were studying her intently. "Yes. Sorry. I didn't mean to wake you."

"I wasn't asleep. Just resting."

"Oh."

"So, what do you have planned for us when we get to San Francisco?" he asked.

"I thought we'd do some sightseeing and a little shopping."

His eyes widened, as if she'd said a bad word. "Shopping?"

"Yes. You've been shopping with me before."

"I know. Don't remind me."

She chuckled. "Was it that bad?"

"No, to be honest, it was worse.

She playfully punched him in the shoulder.

"Hey, take it easy on me, will you? That hurt," he said, rubbing the spot.

"You're a strong man. You can take it."

"Yeah, but it's getting harder and harder for me to take *you,* Dani."

She stared at him, wondering what he meant by that. She parted her lips to ask, and as if he knew what her question would be, he placed his finger to her lips, smiled and said, "Remind me to tell you later."

Danielle felt the elegance of the hotel the moment they walked through the front doors into the spacious atrium, with its marble floors and myriad, healthy-looking, potted plants. As she and Tristan stepped into the elevator, she said, "I hope you don't mind that I got us a suite."

He glanced at her. "Why should I mind? I'm getting used to having you around."

She smiled. "Is that a good thing or a bad thing?"

"It depends, Dani. If you begin talking business it will become a bad thing."

She laughed. "Okay, I promise not to talk business. I even promise not to be in the same room with you whenever you pull out your BlackBerry. But it seems to me that you're the one who's having a hard time remembering we're here to relax."

"I'll relax once that huge Smithfield order leaves the warehouse. We promised them that entire shipment would arrive at its destination by Friday."

"And it will, so chill," she said, easing closer to him when another couple got on the elevator.

"Okay, I'll chill, but I want you to do the same. And if you begin talking about Marc, I'll throttle you. For the next five days I want you to rest and relax and only think of good things."

"Considering how my life has gone lately, that will be hard."

"Try doing so, anyway."

Danielle decided this was not a good time to mention that she had made Alex and Renée promise to keep in touch and let her know if there were any new developments about the fourth woman. When she had told them she would be going to San Francisco for a few days and with whom, they'd seem overjoyed. It was a waste of time trying to convince them that they were barking up the wrong tree with their assumptions about her and Tristan, but she figured now that they had men in their lives they were desperately trying to find someone for her. She was genuinely happy for Alex and Renée and was glad what Marc had done hadn't left any permanent scars.

And she did intend to get on with her new life once she brought closure to her past. Men had a tendency to hit on her all the time, and lately, since word had gotten around that she was a widow, they'd become a little bold. She was grateful that, thanks to Chris, the media hadn't gotten wind of what Marc had done. The tabloids were always looking for a way to link her with someone, but after she'd married Marc they figured there was nothing new and exciting in her life and had pretty much left her alone for the past five years. If only they knew.

She glanced over at Tristan and knew that one of the reasons men weren't hitting on her more was him. The two of them were always together, and a number of people had the same assumption as Alex and Renée that something was going on between them.

She had mentioned this to Tristan a few times, not wanting those rumors to ever ruin things between him and a woman. He'd told her not to worry about it and to let people think whatever they wanted.

She figured he wasn't all that concerned because he wasn't dating anyone exclusively now. As far as she knew, he wasn't dating at all. She would probably be the first to know, since she hung out with him so much. At night he was at home with her and when he went out, it was with her. No wonder people thought something was going on between them.

Maybe, she thought now, it was a subject she should broach with him again. "Tristan?"

"Yes?"

Her gaze immediately latched on to his lips. They were full, inviting. She felt a sudden pull in her stomach. She wondered how they would feel if she were to press hers against them.

"Dani?"

She snatched her gaze from his lips and focused on his eyes. His probing eyes. "What?"

"You called me. What did you want?"

Frowning, Danielle compressed her lips, deciding for the moment to keep her mouth closed or else she might say the wrong thing.

There was no way she would tell him that for a crazy moment she had been almost ready to ask if she could sample his lips. Almost.

"Dani? What's wrong?"

If only he knew. She glanced up at him and at the other people on the elevator and leaned over and whispered, "It's nothing major. We can talk about it later."

He looked at her as if confused. "All right."

And then she felt it. He had caught hold of her hand and lightly squeezed her fingers. As always, that was his way of letting her know that things would be fine. Of course, that was easy for him to convey—he hadn't been privy to her thoughts. If he'd known what she was thinking he would probably run in the opposite direction.

Contrary to what some people wanted to believe, Tristan was not attracted to her. He thought of her as a kid sister and nothing more. She knew all about that promise he'd made to Paul to watch out for her. That had been why she'd eloped with Marc and hadn't told Tristan until it was over. There was no doubt in her mind that he would have found a way to stop the wedding, convince her she was acting irrationally. Now, considering everything, she wished he *had* intervened. She wouldn't be in this predicament.

The elevator door whooshed open, and she and Tristan stepped off. He continued to hold her hand as they walked down the long hallway.

"I was able to get tickets for that train ride through Napa Valley tomorrow," he said.

She smiled at him. "That sounds wonderful. It's a while since I've been in this area. I'd also like to cross the Golden Gate Bridge to Sausalito."

"That won't be a problem."

As they continued walking down the hall toward their suite, she couldn't help but get excited about the next five days they would be spending together.

Tristan began unpacking his clothes and putting them away. The suite was even nicer than he'd thought it would be. Two bedrooms and a common living area, it was roomy, spacious and just what he and Dani needed. As much as he wanted to spend time with her, he didn't want to cramp her space.

Actually he had been surprised that she had insisted he come along. He had wanted her to take time away, thinking she needed to be by herself. But then, almost too late, he'd realized that any man in his right mind wouldn't send a woman who looked like Danielle off on a vacation alone. The moment they had walked into the hotel lobby it seemed that the eyes of every single male in the place were drawn to her.

When he heard a knock, he crossed the room to the door that connected to the suite's living room. He opened it to find Danielle standing there in a printed, flyaway cover-up with a matching bikini underneath. He forced his gaze off the outfit, above her exposed stomach, and up to her face. "Going to the pool?"

She smiled. "Yes, and I wanted to see if you'd like to join me."

"I'm still unpacking."

"Boy, you're slow. One of the first things you learn as a model is the correct way to pack so you can unpack easily. I'm going to have you show you how it works one of these days."

She glanced around him to see his room. "It looks like mine."

He opened the door wider. "Come on in. If you don't mind waiting for minute, I'll join you in that swim."

"Sure," she said, entering the room when he moved aside. She immediately crossed to the window.

Tristan's gaze roamed over her and the outfit she was wearing. He was glad she had agreed to wait for him. There was no way he wanted her anywhere near the pool without him.

"Hey, wait a minute. You have a better view of the Bay. That's not fair."

He chuckled as he went about placing his shirts on hangers. "Stop whining. I'll swap if you want," he offered. *Or you can just stay in this room with me if you prefer.* He wanted to say it but he didn't.

"That's okay," she said, grinning. "I'll let you keep this one pleasure in life."

He glanced over at her, saw her beauty

against the backdrop of the view outside the window and thought there couldn't be any pleasure greater than loving her. "Have you decided what we're going to do for dinner?"

She left the window to sit on his bed. "The restaurant downstairs looks nice. Why don't we eat there tonight?"

"That's fine with me. I'm going to step into the bathroom to put on my swim trunks and will be back out in a second."

"All right."

And then he disappeared, putting a closed door between him and temptation.

"So, what were you going to ask me about earlier on the elevator?"

Danielle glanced over at Tristan. They were lying side by side on loungers by the pool. It was a beautiful July day and a bright sun was in the sky. She thought the swim trunks Tristan wore looked sexy on him. She'd always thought he had a nice body.

Earlier, when she'd gotten up to get drinks for them at the poolside bar, she'd noticed a woman trying to catch his eye. Danielle knew enough about women to know that although the woman had a nice body, she was probably in her fifties. She was definitely a cougar. And Danielle had no intention of letting her get her claws into Tristan. At first the thought of her being so overprotective gave her pause. Hadn't she felt the same way about Karin Stokes? But then she realized Tristan was such a nice guy, someone had to look out for him. There were too many unscrupulous women out there, like the cougar in the lounger on the other side of the pool who was still trying to get his eye. Why didn't the woman just give up?

"Um, I was just wondering," she said, deciding to respond since he had inquired, "why you aren't seriously dating anybody."

He released her gaze to look out over the pool. "I don't have the time."

She grinned. "I thought that was one of the things in life that a man typically made time for. Paul usually did."

Tristan chuckled. "Yeah, he did, didn't he?"

Both of them knew her brother had been a

ladies' man. She and Tristan hadn't been the only ones grieving over his death. A lot of the single ladies in Port St. Lucie had been grieving as well. "So, Tris, what's the real deal?"

Tristan didn't say anything at first, deciding to think about what response he would give Danielle. He could come right out and say he wasn't dating anyone because she was the one and only woman for him. But he reconsidered. Given what she was going through right now and had gone through over the past two months, hearing that would be the last thing she needed. He made his head rule his heart and said, "I've been too busy."

"And I guess I haven't been helping matters."

He frowned. "I thought we weren't going there, Dani. Don't bring *him* on this trip," he said rather harshly and then regretted it.

For once he wanted her to relax and have a good time without thinking of what had been going on in her life for the past couple of months. He knew for her it would be hard to do, but he wanted her to try.

"Sorry."

"You're forgiven."

A few silent moments passed and then she said, "Did I tell you I got a call from Jeri?"

His frown deepened. Jeri had been her agent. More than once the woman had tried luring Danielle back into the world of glitz and glamour. "No, you didn't. What did she want?" he asked, trying to keep the irritation he felt out of his voice.

"A major designer is putting a project together for the holidays and wants me included."

Alarm rammed through his nervous system. He couldn't help wondering if this thing with Marc would be what sent her back to the world she'd left behind five years ago. "What did you tell her?"

"I told her there was no way I could participate. I have a full-time job at A&T."

He appreciated her loyalty to the company and was grateful she wasn't thinking about leaving A&T. To be open-minded and fair, he said, "You know, if you really want to do it, we could arrange things for you to take some time off. It might be a good opportunity for you."

She shifted to her side on the lounger to face him. "Thanks but no thanks. I told you when I came back that I didn't want that type of life anymore. I was burned out, and even if Paul had lived I think eventually I would have returned home."

This was the first he'd heard that. "I thought you enjoyed your career as a model."

"I did at first, but then the long hours, living out of my luggage and barely eating to stay thin ran its course. I had begun to get homesick and it took everything I had to get up each day and pose in front of the cameras."

"Did Paul know how you felt?"

"No, I never told him. I came close to doing so one night when he called, but before I got the chance he told me about his orders to go to Iraq. Now I'm glad I never told him. You know Paul. He would have left worrying about me."

Tristan didn't want to tell her that Paul had worried about her, anyway. That was one of the reasons he'd asked Tristan to look after her if anything was to happen to him. Paul had also been proud of her. Tristan would never forget the time Dani made the cover of the *Sports Illustrated* swimsuit edition. Paul had purchased all the magazines off the rack at one particular store to give copies to their customers.

"Are you really happy working at A&T, Dani?"

"Yes, that's the only part of my life I'm enjoying right now. I feel close to Paul there. The business was his dream and when you told me he left his share of the business to me, I was deeply touched. I know how hard the two of you worked to make the company a success. I like handling new accounts and watching sales increase, and making sure we're meeting those companies' needs and doing whatever we can to better serve them."

Tristan nodded. She was smart and did an excellent job; she'd become a real asset to the company. But then, he'd figured she would. He'd had no qualms about her taking over for Paul.

He saw her smother a yawn and knew she was probably tired. It had been a long flight, they were now in Pacific time but their bodies were still thinking Florida time.

"Do you want to take a nap before dinner?"

She smiled. "I think I will. Do we need to make reservations for dinner?"

"Yes. I'll take care of it."

"Thanks."

He watched as she stood and covered her bikini with the cover-up. "What time do you want me ready and dressed for dinner?"

"Um, how about around six?"

"That'll work."

He stood, as well, and together they began walking toward the door that led to a bank of elevators. When he placed his hand at the small of her back, he actually felt heat there. And he couldn't help but look forward to dinner with her later.

Chapter 3

Once Danielle had changed out of her bathing suit and slipped on comfortable lounge wear, she contacted Alex and Renée.

Alex answered, seemingly more alert than she had been the last time they'd spoken. The same thing with Renée. When both women said they were alone and their men hadn't come in from work, Danielle appreciated the difference in time zones.

"Has either of you discovered anything

else?" she asked, dropping into the love seat in her room.

"Before we answer that, we want to know how things are going in San Francisco. How is Tristan?"

Danielle rolled her eyes, knowing why they were asking. "That's not the issue here, ladies."

"We think it is, Danielle," she heard Renée say. "We're worried about you. We care."

She couldn't help but be touched. Over the past two months, they had endured a lot together, had felt the same pain, had been cut by the same deceit. Only difference from her was that they had moved on and had lives.

But she mustn't allow herself to dwell on that right now. The most important issue, the most pressing issue was the fact that there was another person out there somewhere, another of Marc Foster's victims. That was what she had to focus on.

"I'm fine, really. You don't have to worry about me. I'm tough. I can hang. Tristan is a good friend. He's always been there for me and I appreciate him."

When neither women said anything, especially Alex, who was usually upbeat, Danielle got a funny feeling in the pit of her stomach. What were they trying to prepare her for? "You *have* found out something," she said slowly, almost certain of it. "What is it?"

When neither said anything for a moment, her throat tightened, a sign of anxiety creeping in. "Hey, don't hold back on me now."

It was Renée who finally spoke. "We don't want to ruin your vacation with Tristan."

"You won't. I feel relaxed."

"What we'll tell you won't let you relax, Danielle. It's going to make you mad. It made *us* mad."

Her head began spinning, wondering what they knew. "Let me be the judge of that. I'm a big girl. Finding out that Marc was sterile came as a big blow. I'm thirty. Your biological clock hasn't started ticking. Mine has. I hear it every day."

"But you have Tristan," Alex said.

Danielle felt her heart stir a little. Yes, she had Tristan, but not in the way they thought.

And she knew it would be a waste of time trying to convince them of it yet again. She and Tristan were best friends, nothing more.

Still, she couldn't help but think of a little girl with Tristan's dimpled smile. She suddenly closed her eyes, as if to blink away the image, and felt annoyed with herself. How could she think such a thing? Then again, she knew Tristan was a giver. He would give her a baby if she asked him….

She felt the pulse beat erratically in her throat. No, she couldn't do that. Tristan had given her too much of himself already. She couldn't—she wouldn't—ask him for more. It wouldn't be fair.

"Yes, I have Tristan," she said, although she knew their meaning of that was different from hers. "Now tell me what the two of you have found out."

"You tell her, Renée," Alex said.

"Okay, but Chris won't like me telling you, although I think he'll actually be relieved, since he wouldn't know how to tell you himself. He had a hard time telling me, and I'm sure Hunter had a hard time telling Alex."

Danielle felt like pulling her hair out. "Tell me what?"

"Just what Chris found at Marc's apartment and why he thinks there's another woman, a fourth woman."

Danielle's throat tightened again. "What did he find?"

Renée hesitated a moment before continuing. "The apartment was spacious and it had four bedrooms. A bedroom for each of us."

Danielle felt her skin crawl and tried to subdue the feeling. "What do you mean?"

"What she means is this," Alex said, taking up the story. "We each had our own room and they were furnished with each of us in mind. Decorated in our favorite colors and on the dressers were our favorite perfume, bath oil and even a listing of our favorite foods and hobbies. In the closets were items of our clothing he had obviously collected along the way. And in the bathroom were bathrobes with each of our names embroidered on them. Each room, according to what Chris told Hunter, was a shrine to each of us."

Danielle didn't say anything, mainly because she didn't know what to say. To be quite honest, she doubted she could find her voice to speak, considering how taken aback she felt by what Alex and Renée had just shared. She couldn't help but wonder how a man could marry three women, three different types of women, and then establish rooms under one roof for all of them. What kind of mentality would do such a thing? A question suddenly formed in her mind.

"What about the fourth room? The one belonging to the other woman?" she heard herself asking.

"It wasn't complete. There were several things missing in hers that we had in ours," Renée said. "That's why Chris thinks he hadn't married her yet. Your room, Danielle, according to Chris, was more furnished than mine, and mine had more stuff in it than Alex's. It seemed he was still collecting items for the fourth woman. No items of clothing, no personal effects. He had collected a few menus from restaurants the two of them must have gone to together, but Chris won't tell me what those places are or where they are."

Danielle heard what Renée was saying. And she knew that now, more so than ever, she needed to find the woman to make sure she wasn't wondering why Marc hadn't yet come back to her.

Danielle inhaled deeply. "Okay. I hope Chris shares more with me and Tristan when we meet with him in a few days."

"We're looking forward to your visit," Renée said in an excited voice. "And no matter what we've shared with you, Danielle, you have to get beyond it like we've gotten beyond it. You have to believe there is life beyond Marc."

"I do." She felt the need to say it, although she knew that she hadn't made an effort to pursue that life.

"Then act like it. We can understand you wanting to bring closure to everything, but we don't want you to get so obsessed that you forget something important."

"What?"

"Marc is dead. He can't hurt us anymore.

But you, Alex and I, as well as Mystery Woman Number Four, are alive. And it's time for you, Danielle, to start living."

It's time for you to start living....

With a deep inhalation of breath she forced down the anxiety she felt. Alex and Renée were right. She needed to start living, but knew she wouldn't be able to until she brought closure to her life with Marc. She wished there was another way, but she knew there wasn't.

She moved away from the window where she'd been standing since ending her phone call with Alex and Renée ten minutes ago. A part of her wanted to lie down and rest, but she couldn't do that, either.

She wanted to talk to Tristan.

But how could she when she couldn't let him know she had spoken with Alex and Renée? He would see that as letting this thing with Marc intrude on time when she should be relaxing. He would be upset.

Still, she wanted to see him. He was her best friend and even if she couldn't let him know that something was bothering her, just being around him would calm her troubled mind.

Leaving her bedroom, she crossed the sitting room and saw his bedroom door was slightly ajar. She was about to knock when she noticed him stretched across the bed, asleep. That was when she remembered they had both left the pool area with the intention of returning to their rooms for a nap.

She started to turn around and then decided that since she felt the need to be close to him, she would lie down beside him. If he were to wake up and find her there, he would know something was bothering her but wouldn't ask any questions. He would wait for her to tell him.

The same thing had happened one night after Paul had died. She had spent the night at Tristan's place and had had a bad dream about Paul's death. In her nightmare she'd seen the helicopter crash that had taken him from her.

She had awakened in tears and had somehow made it to Tristan's room. He had been sound asleep and she had eased into bed beside him. He had eventually awakened and found her there. Instead of asking why she'd gotten into his bed, he had held her for the rest of the night.

The next morning she'd told him what had sent her scurrying to his room, and he'd told her then that he would always be there if she needed him. Well, she needed him now.

Slipping off her sandals, she slid into bed next to Tristan and suddenly felt a moment of peace and calm. Satisfied that he was near, she closed her eyes, and moments later she felt herself drifting off to sleep.

Something woke Tristan and he immediately knew what it was. Danielle's scent. She had been using the same perfume for as long as he could remember, and now it was reaching out to him, teasing his nostrils.

He shifted in bed and his leg touched something. It was someone else's leg. A smooth, feminine leg. A long leg. A very shapely leg. He opened his eyes and saw Dani sleeping beside him. He sucked in his breath. The very fact that she was here in bed with him made his entire body ache, but he willed his body to calm down and relax while wondering what had driven her out of her bedroom into his.

He decided not to wake her up to find out. This wasn't the first time she'd sought out his bed when something had disturbed her sleep. He liked the fact that she knew she could come to him when things in her life weren't going the way they should.

He gave a mental shrug, wondering exactly what that did for him. Well, for one thing, it made him feel needed, because she knew that he would always be there for her. It would always be that way between them, although deep down a part of him wanted more.

Her body shifted and as he continued to watch, she opened her eyes and looked up into his. He felt his gut tighten when she moistened her lips.

"I guess you're wondering what I'm doing in here," she said softly.

Her words, Danielle noted, had been met with silence. The other thing she noticed was the intensity of Tristan's gaze. She felt her heartbeat speed up and wondered for a moment why that was. What was making her suddenly feel that she was the object of his desire? And why was her body responding to that very thought?

She frowned, finding such a thought confusing, as well as downright ridiculous. Alex and Renée's false assumptions were getting to her, messing with her mind at a time when she needed to keep things together.

"So since you're the one who brought it up, do you want to tell me why you're in my bed?"

She briefly looked away, mainly because his dark eyes were unwavering and caused parts of her body to stir in a way they hadn't stirred before. She reflected on that for a moment and then shrugged, thinking she was misinterpreting things.

This was Tristan. The man who had always been a part of her life. The man who had been her brother's best friend. The man who was *her* best friend now. The last thing she wanted was to become some hopeless case. She'd be damned if she'd let her need for more in her life, her hunger for the same kind of love, affection and attention Alex and Renée were receiving, cause her to ruin her and Tristan's very special friendship.

"Dani?"

Determined not to let a sudden case of deprived hormones wreck what they shared, she forced a smile. "Would you believe I had a bad dream?"

He smiled. "I'll believe whatever you tell me. But remember, I can catch you in a lie even on my bad days."

Yes, he could. Although she didn't want to admit the truth to him, she knew she had to. She couldn't hold inside the emotions tearing at her. So she pulled herself up in bed and looked over at him. It took all her willpower not to study the wide expanse of his chest somewhat exposed by the tight muscle shirt he'd changed into when he'd returned to his room. And she'd thought his abs had looked fine in the T-shirt he'd worn at the pool.

She gave herself a mental shake and brought her attention back to the matter at hand. She had told him that she would enjoy this time away and not think about Marc and what he had done. But she *had* thought of those things. Tristan wasn't going to like it. Clearing her throat, she began. "I talked to Alex and Renée."

His eyes didn't blink when he asked, "When?"

"Um, about an hour or so ago."

"And what they said made you come and climb into bed with me?"

She broke eye contact with him. "Yes. What they said bothered me."

He didn't say anything for a few seconds. Then he spoke in a calm voice. "I thought you were not going to let Marc stop you from having a good time."

She met his gaze. "Oh, Tristan, honestly I tried. But I won't be able to move on until there's closure." She paused and then said, "They told me about Marc's apartment and what Chris found."

When he didn't appear the least interested in knowing what Chris had found, she could make only one assumption. "You knew, didn't you?" she asked in a soft yet accusing voice. "Chris told you."

"Yes, he told me."

Danielle frowned. "That's just great!" she said sarcastically. "Why didn't you tell me?"

He pulled himself up in bed, as well. "I told you all you needed to know for the time being. You would have learned about the rest when we met with Chris next week. By then you would have enjoyed a few days without worrying about anything. That's what I wanted for you, Dani."

He sounded so impassioned and sincere about it that she really couldn't get mad at him. And she knew that he was and always would be that way when dealing with her. Protective. He was the one male she knew she could count on and totally trust. He had come through for her so many times.

"I know that's what you wanted," she heard herself say. "I guess a part of me wanted that, too. I desperately need time to reconstruct my self-esteem. But then another part, the one that can't fully move forward, knows that as long as there are loose ends out there, I can't do that. And there is a loose end out there, Tris."

As they stared at each other, he fully understood the extent of her determination, the pain driving her motivation and the degree of her fortitude to fix Marc's wrongs.

"Okay," he finally said. "What do you need me to do, Dani? How can I lessen the load?"

For a heartbeat she considered telling him that what he could really do for her was take the edge off. Lately they'd been spending a lot of time together, and just now being around him—friend or not—was reminding her of the way things could be between a man and woman. She recalled the playfulness in Alex's voice that morning last week when Hunter had been vying for his wife's attention, and the breathlessness she'd heard in Renée's voice when she'd answered the phone that morning. It hadn't taken much for Danielle to guess that she'd probably interrupted Renée and Chris's private time together.

Lovemaking was something she hadn't indulged in for quite a while. There could be a lot said for lack of companionship or not having a lover. She had begun getting accustomed to Marc not being around and had almost made up her mind to purchase one of those mechanical toys. But she had talked herself out of doing so, thinking she wasn't that hard up for a man. Now she had to admit that it was a possibility, since lately she couldn't discount her intense attraction to Tristan. He was a good-looking man, and being attracted to him could mean only one thing. She was in desperate need of a sexual fix. Was that something one friend could ask of another?

Her heart began thumping erratically in her chest. Tristan was her friend, her very best friend, and he'd always been there for her to give her whatever she needed. Would he agree to cross the line if what she needed was something of a sexual nature?

"Dani? What's going on in that pretty little head of yours? Tell me. Is there anything I can do?"

Sighing deeply, she shook her head. Then

something within her pushed her to come clean. "You've really done enough. But since you asked, there is this one little thing."

"All right. What is it?"

She braced herself for what his reaction would be and said, "I'm in desperate need of a lover. Would you be it?"

Chapter 4

Tristan took a deep breath as he struggled to retain his composure. Did she really mean what she was asking for? He knew she was not a child. She was a woman with needs, needs she could define, and it seemed she had clearly identified hers.

He studied her face and saw the embarrassing tint she couldn't hide. He knew it had probably taken a lot to ask something like that of him. He realized, too, just how difficult things must be for her. He knew horniness was no joke, since he'd been afflicted by it a few times. He'd always figured Dani was a sensual and passionate woman, and the last thing she'd needed had been a man who hadn't delivered, like the asshole she'd married.

Believing that the best relationships started with friendship, he kept his voice steady when he said, "Um, what's your definition of 'lover'?" He needed to make sure they were on the same page and wanted the same thing.

She didn't say anything for a few moments and then she spoke in a voice that sounded raspy. "A lover is someone you sleep with."

"You just slept with me. Would that make us lovers?"

She rolled her eyes. "Oh, for heaven's sake, Tristan, you know what I mean, so stop playing around and—"

She suddenly found herself tumbled on her back. He loomed over her. "Trust me, Dani, I'm not playing around."

And then he captured her mouth with his. On her startled gasp he curled his tongue around hers and took total control of her mouth as he moved forward into a heated kiss. Immediately passion flared as their tongues dueled not for possession but in desperation to appease the hunger both of them felt. It was an expression of need, want and desire all wrapped up in one, and something he thought had taken too long to come. She looped her arms around his neck and he was well aware that this was what he dreamed about every night, what he thought about most of his days. A willing Danielle in his arms, not as his friend, but as his lover.

He knew he had to pull back or he'd have her naked in a heartbeat. On a ragged groan he pulled his mouth from hers and watched how she swiped a tongue over her lips as if she missed the taste of him already.

"You said that you were desperately in need of a lover," he said, trying to get his breathing under control. "I hope that kiss proves you're not the only one. It's been quite a while for me and—"

"Why?" she interrupted him by asking.

"Why has it been a while? Why haven't you been seeing anyone?"

Tristan knew that her question was the perfect opening to confess that he hadn't been seeing anyone because he had fallen in love with her and didn't want anyone else. A part of him felt that maybe he should be upfront with her and tell her how he felt now. But another part of him wasn't sure she was ready for anything as deep as that sort of confession. The last thing he wanted to do was make things awkward between them, do something to make her draw away. Right now her concentration was mainly on satisfying her physical needs. The reason she had come to him was she knew he would do anything and everything for her. She had no idea of the emotion that drove him to do so now.

Deciding to answer her question, he said, "I've been too busy to date anyone, Dani. You of all people should know that. Besides, too many women have marriage on their minds. They want a ring before the relationship even gets going good. I'm not ready to settle down."

He was lying, saying what sounded good coming from a bachelor, even though he would marry her in a heartbeat if the opportunity presented itself. He knew he had her convinced when she nodded as if what he'd said made sense.

"Like I was saying before you interrupted," he continued, "sex for me is something that's out of sight, out of mind. I have a very strong sexual appetite and I'm afraid that if I get it back into my system I'll want it all the time. Could you handle that, Dani? Could you handle me wanting to make love to you all the time?"

He saw how her eyes darkened. He saw how she nervously swiped her bottom lip with her tongue. His gut tightened seeing it. Then she said softly but with strong conviction, "Yes, I could handle it."

He studied her for a moment, felt his body begin to throb. He knew she could handle it, as well, since she'd done a damn good job on that kiss a few moments ago. Besides, she was the only woman who could handle him, because she was the only one he wanted.

"We've been friends for a long time, Dani, and over the last five years we've become the best of friends. Becoming intimate might be awkward for us at first, so I suggest we not rush into anything and just let nature take its course. Just let it happen."

"When?"

He smiled at the anxiousness he heard in her voice. "We'll both know when the time is right."

From the look on her face he wasn't sure she was fully buying what he said, but he knew that she wouldn't push the issue. "Now, I think we should get dressed for dinner, don't you?" he asked.

She eased off the bed and he did likewise. And then he pulled her to him and hugged her tight. "I told you that I would take care of you and I will. Even *that* way, Dani." He brushed a kiss across her lips. "And you won't be disappointed."

While getting dressed for dinner, Danielle replayed her conversation with Tristan over and over in her mind. She had asked him to be her lover and he had agreed to do so only after making sure she knew what it would entail. If his kiss was anything to go by, she knew he would give her just what she wanted. And if he thought he was scaring her off by telling her about his ferocious sexual appetite, he thought wrong. Someone with a ferocious sexual appetite was exactly what she needed. And just like she said, she could handle him. Evidently he wasn't fully convinced of that, so she needed to prove him wrong.

Dressed in her bra and a thong, she walked over to the closet and selected the dress she had sent out to get pressed earlier. A black, slinky minidress was just what she needed tonight to feel sexy and to turn the heat up a notch. Tristan had underestimated her.

Smiling, she pulled the dress off the hanger and slipped into it, working the zipper up in the back. The short hemline was meant to show off her shapely legs, and the deep V neckline was meant to show off her full breasts. A pair she'd always been proud of because they were full, firm and real.

She had to admit that it seemed strange setting Tristan up for seduction, but she had given fair warning and he had agreed to be her lover. She figured making love with him once or twice ought to take care of things.

Walking back over to the bed, she stepped into the pair of black leather toe-strap sandals that complimented her outfit. She had put on her makeup earlier and just needed to apply her lipstick. She remembered how during her early modeling days she would get pumped up and excited when any photo shoot came her way. Now the only thing she wanted coming her way was Tristan.

She crossed the room to the dresser and picked up a sample packet of Arouse, a new cologne one of her modeling friends had sent her a few weeks ago. She dabbed it on a few places on her body thought of as passion points, not actually smelling anything. It was said to work off your body's chemistry and only a man could pick up the enticing scent from a woman. One whiff was supposed to stir a man's blood, rob him of his senses

and make him think of only one thing—
making love.

She heard a door click shut and knew
Tristan had come out of his bedroom into the
sitting area to wait for her. Things were definitely looking a lot brighter than the gloom
she had encountered earlier today while
talking to Alex and Renée. She intended to
spend the rest of her vacation days putting everything out of her mind and enjoying herself.

After finding out the depth of Marc's
betrayal, she had wondered if she would ever
become involved with a man again. She
figured if anything, she would be overly
cautious when the time came. The only reason
she felt at ease now was that the man was
Tristan. Alex and Renée thought she and
Tristan had something going on, anyway, so
they might as well make it real.

Taking one last look at herself, she headed
for the door.

Tristan glanced at the clock on the wall as
he picked up a magazine from the coffee table.

He was a few minutes early, so he sank into the sofa and got comfortable, stretching his long legs out in front of him. He couldn't get out of his mind the conversation he and Danielle had shared. She had actually come out and asked him to be her lover. He intended to oblige her, but only when he felt the time was right. She was in lust. He was in love. There was a big difference and one he wanted her to become aware of. The only thing that concerned him was whether their friendship was up to the test. What if, no matter what, she only wanted friendship from him, friendship and a little bump-and-grind thrown into the mix every once in a while? What if this thing with Marc had affected her in such a way that she didn't want to have a serious relationship with a man ever again?

He rubbed his hand down his face, refusing to give in to the what-ifs. He intended to show Danielle that with the right man she could have it all—a bed partner, a best friend, a loyal mate and a man who wanted to give her everything, including the family she desired. But he couldn't tell her any of that. They were things she needed to find out on her own.

Like the kiss they had shared. There was no way she didn't know that she could turn him on, that he was attracted to her. It was a fact he could no longer hide. During that kiss they had melded their lips together in a lock so tight, he hadn't wanted to separate in order to breathe. What he had wanted to do was position his body over hers and become the lover she craved. The one she said she needed. Never had kissing a woman sent his senses spinning the way kissing Danielle had. He had savored the taste of her all the way to his bones.

And she had responded in kind, just like he had wanted her to, like he had dreamed so many times that she would. For that brief moment, she had forgotten all about what she had gone through lately, what Alex and Renée had shared with her, and all the emotions she had bottled up inside of her. She had let herself go. She had allowed herself to feel and get as caught up in the moment as he had.

Moments later he rose to his feet when he

heard Danielle's bedroom door opening. He had made dinner reservations at a restaurant the hotel concierge had recommended. It was supposed to be the city's best steakhouse, and Tristan was eager to sink his teeth into a juicy T-bone.

He leaned over to place the magazine back on the table when Danielle walked into the room. He glanced up at her and his mouth fell open. It was a wonder that she didn't hear it when it dropped to the floor. He had to catch his breath as his gaze raked over her, up, down and sideways. He wasn't sure which was worse, her dress or her shoes. Both had "Go ahead and take me" written all over them. At that moment the steak was forgotten and more than anything he wanted to sink his teeth into her.

Danielle saw the look in Tristan's eyes and smiled. He'd been taken by surprise, basically caught off guard, and she liked that. Pushing back her hair from her face, she moved across the room to where he stood. "You look nice, Tristan," she said in a voice that had a husky sound to it.

"Thanks. You look nice yourself."

"Thank you."

Tristan looked at her again, taking note of how the material of her short black dress clung softly to her curves and small waist. Earlier he had suggested that they not rush into anything and let nature take its course. From the way his body was responding to her, he could safely say nature was taking its course in a big way.

Then there was the scent of her perfume. There was nothing subtle about the musky fragrance that was doing a number on him, turning up the heat and arousing him a degree higher than he'd ever experienced in his life.

"You ready?"

He met her gaze. "Ready for what?" he asked in a throaty voice.

Her smile widened. "Ready for dinner. What else?"

He stared at her for a moment and then said softly, "You're enjoying this, aren't you?"

"Enjoying what?" she asked innocently, trying to keep the twitch from her lips.

"Making me sweat."

She arched a brow. "Are you sweating, Tris? You look rather calm to me."

"Trust me. In this case looks are deceiving. It wouldn't take much for me to order room service and keep you right here in this room with me."

And to think that he'd thought moving from friends to lovers would be awkward for her. She seemed to be handling it very well. But then, the way she had responded to his kiss earlier should have warned him she didn't need any additional time to warm up to the idea. He had wanted to make sure she understood the implications of what she had asked for. What he'd told her was basically true. He would want to make love to her all the time. He would want as much of her as he could get, everything she would willingly give.

"Come on, let's get out of here," he said, taking her hand and leading her toward the door.

"And if we don't?"

He didn't slow his pace until he made it to the door. Then he stopped and looked at her and said, "If we don't, you're going to find out real quick just how it feels to be taken by a desperate man."

To be taken by a desperate man...

Just the thought sent shivers running down Danielle's spine as she sat across from Tristan at the restaurant. And knowing that the subtle threat had come from his mouth made getting through dinner difficult. They had shared more meals together than she could count. But never before had they dined together while she wondered how it would feel to make love to him.

She didn't want to make things uncomfortable for Tristan, though. Opening up and letting him know of her needs had been serious enough. Now he knew what she wanted and she was pretty convinced he would eventually give it to her. However, it was up to her to make sure he didn't get cold feet or drag things out.

She glanced across the table at him and almost lost her breath when his eyes caught hers in a heart-stopping gaze. It didn't seem real for her to encounter these types of vibes. The chemistry. Where had it come from? Had it been there all the time but she just never realized it? Or was she noticing it now simply because of her own physical needs?

So many questions with no answers, at least not any that she could provide. She was seeing Tristan through different eyes and couldn't help wondering when those eyes had opened. And why.

"What are you thinking about, Dani?"

His voice, low and seductive, stirred something inside of her, made heat settle in certain parts of her body. "I was thinking about us, Tristan, and what brought us to this."

He lifted a brow. "To what? Dinner?"

She knew he was teasing her. He fully understood what she was trying to say. "No, what brought us to sitting here, trying to kill time until we get back to our hotel room, and then wondering what will happen when we do."

"I already know what will happen when we do."

She did, too, and the thought sent heat

through her body. "What happened to your suggestion about not rushing into anything and letting nature take its course?"

He smiled. It was a nice smile that went from one corner of his lips to the other, making her fully aware of him and his mood. "What happened was that killer dress you're wearing. I'm looking forward to taking it off you."

Danielle was glad their table was in a secluded spot, far away from others. She would have hated for anyone else to have heard what he'd just said. He was bold and deliberate, and she liked it. "And I'm looking forward to taking your clothes off, as well."

She saw the way his eyes darkened, noted the hand that moved to pick up his wineglass and watched his mouth as he took a sip. Tonight was a night of awareness, responsiveness and total focus. She didn't intend to miss a thing.

"So, what do you want to talk about other than the two of us getting each other naked when we get back to the room?" he asked in a husky tone.

She smiled, liking the thought of that. "I guess we can talk about what happened to bring us to this point."

He raised a brow. "You asked me to be your lover. I would say that was good starting point."

"Yes, but I really wasn't sure you would go along with it."

"Why not?"

"Because of our friendship."

He didn't say anything for a moment. Then, "It's because of our friendship that I feel comfortable doing it. There's nothing I wouldn't do for you, Dani. I think you know that. Besides, I understand the workings of the human body. You're a grown woman who knows what she wants and what she needs. And I also know what you've been going without. I'm glad you turned to me and not someone else."

Her lips curved into a smile. "To be honest, I hadn't thought of going to anyone. My first inclination was to purchase a...a toy. But then..."

When she hesitated, he inquired, "But then what?"

She waited for the flutters to cease in her stomach before saying, "But then I remembered how deep our relationship goes, and how comfortable we are with each other. Some might see what I've asked of you as taking advantage of our friendship, but I know it's not that at all. Although I wasn't sure what your response would be, a part of me felt comfortable asking."

Tristan didn't say anything. Instead, he thought of how many agonizing nights he had lain in his bed after she'd married, knowing he had lost her, yet knowing he had to find it in his heart to want what was best for her. He'd wanted her to be happy, even if that happiness was with another man.

Nothing had changed in that regard. He still wanted her to be happy. If he could take away what she'd had to endure for the past couple of months, he would. There was no way he could undo the past, but what he could do was build on the future. One step at a time. He would give her the time she needed and would be by her side when she finally brought closure to this complicated part of her life. Then he would become a part of her life in the way he'd wanted for a long time.

He knew what his own needs were, but he'd hold them at bay to take care of hers. She didn't know it, but his went deeper than just the physical. They would never get worked out of his system no matter how many times they made love, simply because it wasn't just an itch he needed her to scratch. It was something so monumental it was almost overpowering. It was so deep that the bottom seemed endless, and so strong he felt like Samson on one of his better days, before his hair had been cut.

"How would you feel if I suggest we forgo dessert?" he asked, knowing she would get his meaning. He felt the sensual heat of her gaze when it touched his face.

"I was going to get a slice of key lime pie. It's my favorite."

A smile touched his lips. "I know. But I promise to give you something just as good."

Their gazes held. "Just as good?" she asked as if intrigued by his claim.

"Yes." And at the risk of sounding rather cocky, he gave her a level look and said, "Key lime pie has nothing on what I'm prepared to give you."

She smiled and felt the slow stirring of heat between her legs. "You have me convinced. I think we should leave now."

"And I totally agree with you."

Chapter 5

Although it was July, the night air off San Francisco Bay was cool, so Danielle wasn't surprised when they exited the restaurant and Tristan took off his jacket and placed it around her shoulders. "Thank you."

"You're welcome."

And then they walked toward the car with his arm around her shoulders, which wasn't an uncommon thing for them to do. She couldn't help but reflect on other things they had done that could have put ideas in other people's heads besides Alex's and Renée's.

Port St. Lucie wasn't a huge town and most of the people knew of Paul and Tristan's close friendship, just like they knew of her and Tristan's close friendship. Even Marc had questioned her about it once, and she had explained that Tristan was like a big brother to her. At least he had been at the time. When had that stopped?

"You're quiet."

Tristan's words broke into her thoughts as he opened the car door for her. "I'm just thinking," she said.

When she slid into the seat he bent low to place the seat belt around her, bringing his face close to hers. "About this, I hope." And then he kissed her, just as easy and just as quick. It was over before she could sneak in some tongue time. She was tempted to pull his mouth back to hers, but he had closed her car door and was moving around the car.

When he slid into the driver's seat, she narrowed her eyes at him. "That wasn't fair."

He smiled as he switched on the engine. "What was unfair about it?"

"Too short."

His smile widened as he pulled out of the parking lot. "I'm saving the longer version for when we get behind closed doors."

"Very well, then," she said, finding a comfortable position in her seat. "I plan to hold you to it."

"Trust me, Dani, it will happen."

She believed him, and that was what she thought was the weirdest thing. She and Tristan were always a pair. They had traveled together numerous times and had even shared hotel rooms during most of them. But nothing had ever happened between them. Again she couldn't help but wonder, why now? Part of her believed it had a lot to do with her asking him to be her lover. Since then, things had certainly gotten hot between them. They were contemplating sleeping together as if it was nothing.

Well, to *her* it was certainly something. She had gone without for almost eight months. Marc had been just that neglectful. She had been satisfied with the promise he'd made, so she hadn't nagged him about the times they hadn't been intimate. But now she knew he hadn't been with her because he'd had two other wives to sleep with. How could she not have detected something?

"You okay?"

She glanced over at Tristan. There was no way she was going to tell him what she was thinking. Mentioning Marc might dampen the mood and she didn't want that. So instead, she said, "I was wondering why it took me so long to seek you out as a lover."

He glanced over at her when the car came to a traffic light. "I think the main reason, Dani, was that you were married."

"Before then, when I was single and living in New York. You even came to see me a few times, spent the night at my place."

"Yes, but if you recall most of the times I showed up, Paul was with me. That one time I showed up by myself you were sick."

She nodded, remembering, surprised that he did. "I thought I was going to die."

He chuckled. "It was a toothache. Most people don't die from it, Dani."

"Well, there was more to the story than I was telling at the time."

"You don't say? What else was there?"

She turned toward him. "Because of the toothache, I had to be replaced for a photo shoot by the one person I hadn't wanted to replace me. I think she deliberately wished that toothache on me."

He raised a dark brow. "Boy, that's deep. She must have been a real witch."

She knew he was teasing her, but she didn't care. As far as she was concerned, she was serious. "Yeah, I thought so at the time, but it doesn't matter. She can have all the photo shoots she wants. That's not my life anymore."

There was a lot of traffic flowing in their direction, which caused Tristan to slow down again. Keeping his eyes on the cars in front of him, he asked quietly, "And what do you see as your life now, Dani?"

She gave a small shrug. "First I want to make sure I have one. Once I can finally put the past behind me, then I want to move on. I like what I'm doing at A&T, but I want to do more."

"Like what?"

"I don't know. Possibly start a foundation in Paul's name. He was a big soccer fan, so I might give a soccer scholarship each year to a deserving student who needs it for college."

"That's very generous of you."

She grinned. "It will be generous of you, too, since it's also your money. I wasn't going to just give it out of my share but ours."

"Ours?" Tristan asked, coming to a stop at a traffic light and looking over at her.

She met his gaze. "Yes, *ours.*"

Their gazes held and for some reason she felt there was a deeper meaning in what she had said and she didn't know why. Since she had stepped in after Paul's death, they had always thought of the company as theirs. They were partners, true enough, but she never considered that she had just a share of the company. In her mind it was theirs. Together.

Tristan released Danielle's gaze when

traffic began moving again. He figured she might not have realized the significance of what she'd just said, but he had. Whether they had acted on it previously or not, they had always shared everything, and tonight they would share each other in the most intimate way. He got turned on just looking at her. And he had no idea what perfume she was wearing, but the scent was like an aphrodisiac, making him fully aware of just how breathtakingly sexy she was. Even when she had sipped her iced tea at dinner, he had gotten aroused. Seeing that straw between her lips, watching her suck on it, had sent all kinds of erotic images crashing through his brain. He could imagine those same lips on—

"Tristan?"

Her voice cut into what he was thinking, and it was a good thing it had. He was fully aroused. He glanced over at her as he pulled into the hotel's parking garage. "Yes?"

"I asked whose bed we're sleeping in tonight."

He brought the car to a stop and cut the engine. He shifted his body to give her his absolute attention. "It really doesn't matter, sweetheart, because I can guarantee you that neither of us will get much sleep."

A short while later while riding the elevator up to their suite, Danielle remembered Tristan's words and shuddered in anticipation. Earlier that day, kissing him back had been natural, as if it was something her body had wanted to do for a long time. It had been one of the most mesmerizing things she'd ever done in her life. She was being swept up in a storm of excitement thinking about what was yet to come. If those subtle hints and sex-laced innuendos he'd made all evening were true, then she was in for the time of her life. And for her it was long overdue.

"You okay?"

She glanced up at him. "Yes, I'm fine."

They had stepped out of the elevator and were walking down the long hallway to their room. Tristan was always asking about her well-being; her physical and mental state had always been of concern to him. They still were. He hadn't known just how she would react when she'd discovered the extent of Marc's deceit. A part of her still didn't want to believe it. She just couldn't accept that any man could stoop so low and be so devious. But her dead husband had, and now she felt obligated to clean up the mess he'd left behind. Chris still wouldn't say which of the three wedding bands Marc had choked on. She figured Chris didn't want her, Alex or Renée feeling guilty. If only he knew just how nonguilty she felt. As far as she was concerned, choking on one of the rings seemed like a fitting way for him to go.

"Let it go, Dani."

She snatched her gaze up to Tristan, wondering how he had known what she'd been thinking. As if the question was in her eyes, he said, "Your breathing shifted from calm to turbulent. At first I thought it was for another reason—until I looked down and saw you frown. Whatever you were thinking about him were unhappy thoughts. Let it go. When we cross over that threshold into our room, I want your complete attention. I don't want to compete for it."

"You won't have to," she assured him, trying to redirect her thoughts and dismiss Marc from her mind. She turned her attention to Tristan and what lay ahead. "Other than the fact we won't be getting much sleep, what else do you want to tell me about tonight?" she asked, smiling.

He looked down at her with those dark, intense eyes she'd always thought were gorgeous. "I intend for it to be special."

"And I have no doubt that it will be," she said.

"And for us things will go beyond me satisfying your needs, Dani."

That statement somewhat confused her, since she thought that was the main reason they were doing it. He would be satisfying her needs and she would be satisfying his. They had both admitted to being in desperate need of a lover and had turned to each other because they trusted each other implicitly.

"I don't understand what you mean," she said truthfully.

He smiled at her when they stopped in front

of the hotel door. "That's fine, but one day you will, Dani. I'm going to make sure of it."

She pondered his words and could only come up with one answer and hope she was right. He knew more than anyone what she wanted, what Marc had cheated her out of. Was Tristan hinting at the possibility he would give her the child she'd always wanted?

She would not have asked that of him, no matter how much she wanted to become a mother. Asking him to be her lover had been bold enough, but she knew where to draw the line. However, the sheer excitement of that possibility had her mind racing, her heart overjoyed, to the point that she felt all misty-eyed. She reached out and touched his hand. "It's a baby, isn't it? You're going to give me a baby?"

Tristan blinked, trying to keep the shock of her words from his face. Making a baby with her had been the farthest thing from his mind. He had a wallet packed with condoms to prove it. The subtle hint he'd given her a few moments ago, when he'd said that what they would share would go beyond satisfying their needs, was mainly about the love he felt for her. A love that he had held inside for years. He had wanted her to eventually see that their lovemaking had nothing to do with just enjoying sex together. In his mind they would be making love in the purest sense of the word.

But a baby?

On more than one occasion he had thought about being the one to give her the baby she wanted, especially when he'd seen how discovering Marc had been sterile had left her broken, nearly destroyed her spirit. That's when the idea first took shape in his head and it had stayed locked in the back of his brain. Now she was bringing it to the forefront. Personally he wanted more between them than satisfying needs and making a baby. He wanted her to come to the realization that he loved her. That was what drove him to do whatever it took to make her happy. On the other hand, he knew more than anyone that a baby would make her happy.

He inhaled deeply; deciding not to burst her bubble by telling her that making a baby with her before they got married was not part of his plan. But then, he wasn't ready to tell her exactly *what* his future plans for them were until she got the closure she sought concerning Marc.

He took her hand and brought it to his lips. There was no need to ask her if she was sure she really wanted a baby. But he had to make sure she truly wanted *his* baby. "Do you really want my baby, Dani? What if he or she is born bad-tempered like me?"

He watched her smile. "Tristan, you are the most mild-mannered person I know, and yes, I truly do want your baby. Just the thought of being pregnant fills me with profound happiness and joy."

There was something about her that let him know what he'd always known. She would make any child a good mother. She would make his child a good mother. She'd had a good role model. Her parents, especially her mom had been the best. He had spent many a night over at the Timmonses' house. And when the grandmother who had raised him died when he was in his senior year of high school, it had been the Timmonses who had taken him in. He never knew his father and his mother. They'd been teenagers who, after he was born, only showed up when looking for a handout. Nothing about that had changed, except now when his mother came looking for a handout she usually had some man trailing behind her.

"Aren't we going inside?"

Tristan heard the anxiousness in her voice and couldn't tell whether the thought of them making a baby was the driving force behind it. Did he really care? The answer came quick. No, he didn't. He loved her and wanted to bring peace and happiness into her life. It was happiness that she deserved.

He tried to downplay the trembling in his hand when he inserted the card into the lock. How long had he dreamed of this moment, actually thought it would never come after she'd gotten married? Now it seemed he was being given another chance.

He took a step back so she could walk in

ahead of him. And then he entered and closed the door behind him, locking it.

Danielle wished she knew what Tristan was thinking. She breathed in, detecting the sexual chemistry that was heavy in the air. She no longer wondered how in just a short span of time they could move their friendship to this level. The important thing was that they had. And what had her feeling as if she was floating on air was the thought that with him, she could have the thing she desired most.

"I want to know the name of the perfume you're wearing."

She met his gaze. He was leaning against the closed door with a look on his face that could only be described as downright enticing. Even his smile seemed to be deliberately stroking her.

"Why?" she asked, taking off the jacket he had placed across her shoulders. She held it in front of her, against her stomach, liking the heat she still felt in it.

"The scent. It's different."

A smile touched her mouth. She wasn't

surprised that he had picked up on something, which proved he was a passionate man. "It's called Arouse," she said, watching the darkening of his eyes when she said it. "It's supposed to—"

"No need to explain. I have an idea what it's supposed to do," he said, moving away from the door and walking slowly toward her. Her gaze traveled over him and immediately noticed something.

"And as you can see," he said, coming to a stop in front of her, "it works." He reached out and took his jacket from her and tossed it on the sofa. He then took hold of her hand to bring her body flush against his. "But I would be in this state even if you hadn't put it on."

"Why?"

"Because I ache for you."

Tristan knew Danielle assumed it was an ache that had begun recently, probably just that day. Someday he would let her know that in all actuality, he'd ached for a long time. It was an ache he thought he would never get rid of, but tonight he would.

He regarded her for a long moment, wanting to kiss her, put his hands all over her, trail his mouth across every inch of her skin. He wanted to know the taste of her just like he wanted her to know the taste of him. Going from friends to lovers would be something she wouldn't forget. Neither would he, and he intended to make it so.

"You said earlier today that you're desperate, Dani. I plan to find out just how desperate you are."

Dani stared at him and could feel him pressed against her. His voice had a husky timbre now, one that sent soft chills through her body, while at the same time an enticing warmth flowed through her veins, heated her blood. She wasn't used to such desire, such an ingrained degree of yearning and craving. He wanted to see desperation? She had no problem displaying it to him in living color.

She couldn't remember the last time she'd been intimate, and considering the man she'd been with, she didn't *want* to remember it. She would welcome any new memories Tristan wanted to make. Tonight was their night. Tomorrow would be their day. For however long it lasted, it would be their time.

She took a step back out of his arms. "You want to see desperation, Tristan Adams? I will give you desperation." And before he could react, she reached behind her and with swift fingers undid the catch of her dress. Before he could blink, it slithered down her hips. As a model she'd learned how to get in and out of clothes quickly, and from the look in his eyes she could tell he appreciated that lesson.

She watched his gaze take in all of her, every inch her black-lace, low-cut pushup bra and matching thong didn't cover. His eyes left a heated trail across certain parts of her body and a lingering hot caress on others. The evidence of his arousal was becoming even more prevalent. Deep within her something seemed to break free. She felt her senses unraveling, replaced by a desire to explore everything and anything with this man.

With that thought imprinted in her brain and feeling compelled to get swept up in the storm of emotions that were descending on her like a whirlwind, she took two steps toward him. Instinctively he reached for her, giving her the warm embrace she needed.

Tristan tilted up her face with his fingertips, letting his gaze linger on it for a long moment before slowly lowering his mouth to hers, kissing the sigh off her lips. There he found a sweetness that touched him to the core. He was driven to lap it up with a hunger he felt to his bones. He needed her like he had never needed any other woman, and wanted her just as much.

He heard her moan beneath his mouth while she kissed him back, making his muscles quiver. Simply put, she had a way of igniting passion with fire, the degree of which nearly burned him.

She freed her mouth from his and inhaled deeply, and from the look in her eyes he could tell the kiss had affected her just as much as it had him. He would show her desperation, as well, he thought, taking a step back and kicking off his shoes. Next came his socks and shirt, and he looked at her when he began easing his pants down his legs.

He heard her draw in a shaky breath, and the sound of it sent blood rushing through his veins. Desire, more potent than anything he had ever felt before, filled his mind, made his body tremble in anticipation.

They stood facing each other with nothing separating them but their underwear. A long silence grew between them as they stared at each other and then simultaneously they began removing the last pieces of clothing.

Somehow Danielle managed to remove her bra and thong before Tristan got his boxer shorts down his legs. When he straightened, she was staring at him. Her eyes traveled all over his body, taking in his broad shoulders, muscled arms, the flat plane of his stomach and then that part of him in the middle, huge and aroused.

In return, he couldn't help but take in all of her naked body. The perfect curves of her hips, her firm breasts with the darkened nipples, and especially every detail of her Brazilian wax. Needing to touch her, he took a step forward, reached out and slid his hands over her stomach, her hips, and then firmly clutched her backside, liking the feel of her warm flesh in his hands.

He looked down at her just as she tilted her face to him. From her expression he knew exactly what she wanted. It was the same thing *he* wanted. He lowered his mouth and captured hers, immediately using his tongue to explore her, taste her, gently at first, then more deeply, and finally with an intensity that had him groaning.

Without breaking mouth contact, he swept her into his arms and headed for his bedroom.

Danielle sighed deeply against Tristan's solid chest. She wasn't sure if he was carrying her to his bedroom or hers. At the moment it didn't matter, just as long as he found a bed. Going without for eight months had taken its toll and she needed relief.

She needed him.

She felt the mattress at her back when he placed her on the bed and then stood back and raked his gaze over every naked detail of her body, missing nothing. She felt neither embarrassed nor ashamed at his perusal.

"I want to touch you all over, Dani," he said in a husky voice. "And I want to taste you all over, too."

She rose on her haunches, letting her gaze take in all of him, and said in a low voice, "And I want to touch and taste *you* all over."

He moved closer to the bed and reached out, and the moment he touched her, she felt fire in his fingertips, heating her skin, seeping into her bloodstream, making her want him even more. Mesmerized, she watched the movement of his fingers across her skin, trailing a path upward to her breasts. Then his hands were kneading her there, stroking her and eliciting a need to touch him as intimately.

She reached down and took his erection in her hand, hearing his breath catch when she did so. And then she began stroking him with the same precision he was using on her breasts.

Moments later she felt herself being lowered

to the bed. She looked up as he shifted his body to straddle her before leaning down and capturing a nipple in his mouth.

She let out a long, deep moan and then she felt his hand move to the area between her legs. Her body immediately responded as he painstakingly began stroking her feminine core.

Her breath seemed to get caught in her throat, as if she was fearful of breathing. Tension filled her body, unlike anything she'd experienced in a long time, if ever. She felt on the verge of breaking in two.

"Tristan."

She said his name as the searing impact of what was happening to her hit home. She felt her insides tighten, and then when he let go of her breasts and lifted his head and looked at her, the darkness in his eyes sent emotions riveting through her.

"That was the touch," he whispered in a throaty voice as a slow smile curved his lips. "Now for the taste."

And then before she could blink, he had shifted his body and lowered his head between her legs. He grasped her hips, and the moment he inserted his tongue inside her, she felt boneless, ready to shoot off the bed. But his firm grip on her hips kept her from moving, held her a prisoner beneath his mouth. And she gloried in captivity, felt hot clenching pleasure under his restraints. It seemed as if his tongue went deeper, as if it thickened with the places it touched.

Her hands clutched his shoulders and suddenly she felt her body come apart as she was tossed into a sea of pleasure where wave after wave of ecstasy took her under.

"Tristan!"

She screamed his name as she felt her body break into tiny pieces. But he didn't let up. He didn't let go. At least not until the last shudder passed through her. After lapping her one last time, as if for good measure, he raised his head and licked his lips before easing his body in place over hers. Then, looking deep into her eyes, holding her gaze, he slowly entered her body.

Before she could pull in a breath, he began

moving, stroking her insides with long, hard thrusts, and she suddenly felt the buildup of passion and desire all over again. The tempo of his thrusts increased. It might have been her imagination, but she felt the bed shake, everything begin to spin. The appeasement of desperation had never been so good, so full of fire and physical responsiveness.

He was taking more than she thought she had to give and was giving more than she thought it was possible to receive. And then she heard his throaty growl and felt his body jerk the same moment she felt another explosion rip into her. She screamed, marking his shoulders with her fingernails, but his thrusts kept coming, going deeper and deeper.

When the room finally stopped spinning and the bed stopped shaking, she gave in to sensations that were too numerous to name, but she felt each and every one of them. And she was helpless to do anything but tumble into sweet, sensual oblivion.

Chapter 6

There were very few reasons for Danielle to sleep late on any given morning. Being tired from making love all night had never been one of them.

She could barely open her eyes to glance at the clock on the nightstand, and at the moment she couldn't recall whose bed it was. They had started out in Tristan's bed, but sometime during the wee hours of the morning after they had gotten up to take a bath together in the large Jacuzzi tub, they had ended up in her bed.

"Ready for a few more rounds?"

She shifted her eyes to Tristan. He was lying on his back, totally naked and definitely aroused. He had to be kidding. But the heated look in his eyes told her that he was dead serious. She wondered what kind of vitamins he was taking and somehow found the strength to laugh. "Are you trying to scare me, Tristan?"

He smiled. "Scare you about what?"

"The size. It seems to have gotten bigger."

Now it was Tristan who laughed, not believing the conversation they were having. "You're imagining things, Dani, but there's one way to find out." And before she could blink he had straddled her body, sliding between her legs as if he rightly belonged there.

Tristan heard Danielle's sharp intake of breath when he gripped her hips and nudged her legs apart, then lowered the tip of his aroused shaft very close to the entrance to her feminine core.

"Let's see if it can still get in," he said in a husky voice as he slowly began easing inside of her. Their gazes held as her body automatically stretched to accommodate him.

Danielle held tight to Tristan's shoulders, and what she felt was not discomfort but an immediate stirring of desire and passion. The deeper he entered her, the more she felt the fullness of him. It seemed her senses became aligned with a momentous need that only he could appease. When he sank into her to the hilt, he paused, making her fully aware of just how deep he had gone, how tight the connection. She studied his features—the clenched jaw, the nostrils that were flaring with each breath he took and the dark eyes that bore into her.

"Do you want me to start moving now?" he asked moments later in a voice so low she had to strain her ears to hear it. Gripping his shoulders tighter, she whispered back, "I'd be tempted to hurt you if you don't."

She could tell by the look that touched his features that he was amused. Amused and aroused. From the feel of things that was a fascinating combination. "Hurt me?" At her nod, he couldn't help but ask, "How can you hurt me?"

"Like this, Tris."

She began clenching her inner muscles,

securing him with a strong hold and then releasing him. She did it over and over, and the action had a milking effect on his shaft, as if she was deliberately pulling everything out of it. He found her actions so mind-blowing that he had to remind himself to breathe. He shook his head, trying to retain control of his senses, the same senses that were getting shot to hell each and every time she clenched her muscles. When he was finally capable of speech, he said, "Sweetheart, if this is your brand of torture, then you can torture me anytime. This is definitely the kind of pain I enjoy."

She smiled. "Glad to hear it. Now will you move? The wait is killing me."

In response to her request he began moving, releasing a slow breath with each and every methodical stroke inside her. She took advantage of the rhythm and began moving her hips in a well-blended, near-perfect rotation to his, a mating dance created just for them.

"I wish you wouldn't do that," he said when she moved and then clenched her muscles, moved and then clenched, doing so with agonizing precision, fine-tuned deliberation. If she was priming him for something, what she was doing with her body was one surefire way to ignite the flame inside of him.

He moved his hands under her to lift her bottom for even deeper penetration, seizing the moment to drive her over the edge while knowing he would be following close behind. He felt blood, hot and thick, flow through his veins, especially the ones in his shaft. It felt engorged, close to erupting.

When she began tumbling she screamed out his name and clamped her inner muscles tight around him and then started milking him furiously, with everything she had, demanding everything from him that he had to give. His thrusts increased until suddenly his entire body went off inside her in one gigantic explosion, shooting his seed into the depth of her womb. It was then that she moved her legs to lock hers with his, making sure he didn't go anywhere. He didn't. He stayed put and continued to flood her insides with the very essence of him.

When she shuddered while calling his name, he felt it all the way to his bones. He wanted to mentally absorb it into his brain, spread it through his mind. He couldn't think. He couldn't get enough of her. The only thing he could do was take and give, repeatedly, all over again. It was a simple gesture, a compelling need, and until that very moment, he'd had no idea of the degree of love and passion that a man could feel for a woman.

Holding her close to his heart, he rode the tide of intense satisfaction and fulfillment with her in total abandonment and pure, attainable joy.

"Will you tell me again why we're here and not back at the hotel?" Tristan asked softly.

Dani glanced over her shoulder at him and found she was very close to his face, specifically his lips. She was tempted to stick out her tongue and get a taste, but she couldn't do that, not in a crowded department store.

"I need to pick up something for Renée and Chris's wedding." She then returned to checking out a beautiful porcelain vase.

"I wouldn't buy that if I were you," Tristan said close to her ear again. "Especially if you're thinking about transporting it on the plane."

He was right. She had seen the way their luggage had gotten tossed around at the airport. "That's why we should consider expanding our business out here, Tris."

Right now they were a regional operation, and although they had a number of clients and were doing well financially, she'd always tossed around the idea of expansion and felt it was time to test the waters.

"I know we're here on vacation, but I think we should use the opportunity to check out a few things."

He raised a brow. "A few things like what?"

"The possibility of our buying Shipping Source."

For years Shipping Source had been their rival. It had expanded from the East Coast to the West and had even picked up a few Northern states in the process. The company had been doing extremely well until the owner suddenly passed away. His only son, a professional football player, had no desire to step into his father's shoes and had made the decision to sell the company.

Danielle and Tristan had discussed the possibility of a merger, but news of Marc's death had placed it on the back burner. During the days following Marc's funeral when tension between her, Alex and Renée was high, Renée had threatened to freeze Danielle and Alex's assets until the matter of which of them was Marc's legal wife was settled.

"What do you think, Tris?"

Tristan didn't want to tell her, but he'd thought a lot about it and was glad she was taking the initiative to move on in her life by once again considering such a measure. Buying Shipping Source would be the first step and would show that she was in the business for the long haul. He would be the first to admit that he sometimes wondered if she would want to pursue another profession. He was pretty convinced that she wouldn't return to modeling, but a woman with Dani's looks, personality and brains would be a valuable asset to any business. She was sharp as a tack when it came to business matters. She knew their shipping company inside and out, mainly because Paul had always included her. While she was in college she'd worked for them over the summers, and then later, she would take time off from her modeling career to pitch in during the Christmas holidays, their busiest time.

Those had been some of the best days of Tristan's life. Paul had been with them and they had made one hell of a team. At the end of the day they would retire to their favorite bar-and-grill, and while drinking beer and eating pretzels, Dani would bring them up-to-date on her life as a high-fashion model.

Everyone in the Port St. Lucie community loved her and was proud of her achievements. This was because each time she returned home to them, she was Danielle Timmons, the unaffected local girl who'd made it good but never thought herself better than anyone else.

"What you're suggesting will take up a lot

of our time, Dani," he decided to say. "It will be one hell of a commitment to make."

She met his gaze beseechingly. "I know, but I believe we can do it, Tris."

He believed they could do it, as well, and it would definitely give her something else besides her phony marriage to Marc to focus on. "Okay, then, I'll contact our attorney when we get back."

As they continued walking through the department store, he couldn't help but remember what had transpired between them last night and this morning. He had wanted her with a passion and had taken her that way. They had been good together and he was convinced even she knew it.

When Tristan suddenly noticed they were in the ladies' department of the store, he knew what he was in for. He had gone shopping with Danielle too many times not to know the routine. "I prefer that if you start taking your clothes off, we go back to the hotel."

Her lips twitched. "Yeah, but I won't have a full rack of clothes to try on," she said as if to reason with him.

He studied her for a moment, from the top of her head to her feet. She was wearing a printed V-neck stretched T with an embroidered scalloped-hem skirt of ocean blue, and a pair of taupe strappy sandals on her feet. Without even trying she looked liked a model, someone who should grace the covers of any fashion magazine.

"You don't need a rack of clothes to try on." He leaned closer and whispered, "You can always try me on. I promise you can wear me well."

A sensation suddenly got lodged in his chest as he remembered how many times over the past twelve hours her body had been plastered skin to skin to his. He had been inside her so much that a part of him was thinking it had found a permanent home. He wondered if she thought that once they returned to Port St. Lucie, things would go back to the way they were. Just to make sure they were on the same page, he said, "So, do you want to move into my place permanently when we return home?"

Her expression indicated that he had gotten

her attention. She smiled as if she actually thought he was teasing. "I'm already at your place now more than I'm at home, Tris."

"I know but I don't want you to consider your house on Lisbon Street as home anymore." What he was trying to say was that he didn't want her to consider that house she'd shared with Marc as home.

She shrugged. "To be honest with you, I don't. I haven't mentioned it to you, but I'm thinking of selling it. I want to look for another place. Maybe a condo."

He decided not to argue the point about where she'd live. He knew how to work on her in other ways to change her mind, and they were ways they would both find enjoyable. Now if only he could get her out of this damn store. He looked around and then leaned close again. "Will I be able to go into the dressing room with you for a quickie?"

She chuckled, yet at the same time he noted that her breathing had changed. "A quickie?"

"Um, yes. It's where I'll get you in a very compromising position and make it my business—with very limited time—to get inside of you, making it good for the both of us."

He could tell from the expression on her face that he had given her enough to fantasize about. "It could be something as simple and easy as me taking you against the wall. One, two or possibly three hard thrusts ought to do it."

She licked her lips. "One, two or three?" she asked in a somewhat throaty voice.

"I guess I could go for four, although I really don't think a fourth would be necessary. I promise to make it three good ones— hard and fast."

The look in her eyes told him she was taking in everything he was saying. He inched a little closer to her. "Tell me something."

She swallowed and licked her lips a second time. "What?"

"Are you wearing that turn-me-on perfume again? The one that reaches out to me on a primal level and makes me want to take you anywhere and anytime? The same one that has me fantasizing about tasting you all over?"

Even though she wore both a cami and shirt,

he could see the hardened tips of her nipples. They seemed to be begging to be touched, licked, sucked—just about anything his mouth could do to them.

"No, I'm not wearing that perfume."

He nodded and decided not to say in that case it had to be her own natural scent that was getting to him, turning him on, here of all places, in the middle of a damn department store. "I think we need to get out of here, Dani."

"What?" She blinked.

He smiled. "I said we need to leave here or I won't be held responsible for my actions— which just might make the six-o'clock news."

"But I haven't found gifts for Chris and Renée yet."

"Give them gift cards and give *me* what I want." His voice was relatively calm for a man who was getting more aroused by the minute.

"And what is it *you* want?"

"Honestly," he said smoothly, knowing she had to be asking just for the hell of it. He figured for the past ten minutes or so he had painted a pretty clear picture. But just in case he hadn't, he whispered, "I want you naked in my bed, with me taking you in every way known to man and a few ways that haven't been created yet. But like I said, we can always go into one of those dressing rooms for a quickie."

She broke eye contact with him and began fidgeting with a blouse on a hanger. "I've never had a quickie before."

Knowing the asshole she'd been married to for five years, he could well believe that. "Um, I think you'll find it enjoyable. Let me prove it to you."

She cleared her throat. "Maybe some other time."

"I'm going to hold you to it. You won't know what hit you until it's too late." The sight of Dani's sexy body pinned against a wall with him inside her was something he couldn't erase from his mind.

"I think you're right. We better go," she said, placing the blouse back on the rack. "Besides, that saleslady has been watching us. I believe she thinks we're shoplifters or something."

"Then we're doing the right thing by leaving," he said, taking her hand in his and heading for one of the exit doors.

"I got a question for you," she said when they walked down the sidewalk toward their rental car.

He glanced over at her. "What?"

"What's the opposite of a quickie?"

He smiled. "A slow one."

She nodded. "Like last night and this morning?"

He considered her question. He didn't think there was anything slow about having multiple orgasms. The slowness came if you counted the time in between sessions when you had no other choice but to catch your breath. A lot could be said for savoring such moments. A smile touched his lips. "Yes, just like last night and this morning. I prefer taking the time to savor you, long, hard and slow, but when time is of the essence or if your needs suddenly overwhelm you and you've got to have it right then, a quickie is the best way to go."

* * *

"Hungry?"

Danielle turned from looking out the car window and stared wide-eyed at Tristan. "After that conversation in the department store, how on earth can you even think about food?"

He chuckled. "Being aroused has nothing to do with an empty stomach. Besides, we'll both need our strength."

Danielle turned to look back out the car window. Ever since he'd painted a vivid picture of them making love again, her body had gotten set in a ready-to-take-him-on mode. She figured they'd be heading straight to the hotel and making no stops along the way. Evidently she'd been wrong.

"And I perform better on a full stomach."

She decided not to glance back over at him when she said, "That's nice to know."

She had no reason not to believe him since he had certainly outdone himself last night after returning to the hotel from dinner. He had definitely been on top of his game. She had heard how some men had unlimited stamina, but she had never encountered such a man until last night. For a while she'd felt totally out of her depth with him, but he had made her feel a part of everything they'd done. Being taken by a desperate man had been everything she'd fantasized it would be.

"For a renowned fashion model, you've lived a pretty sheltered life."

Tristan's words broke into her thoughts, and she couldn't help but smile at him. "Well, I have to admit I felt like a fish out of water when I made it to New York. It was so different from Port St. Lucie. So fast-paced. Nevertheless, I had no intention of being wild and loose. But then, you can't believe everything you read in the papers about models."

"I never have. I always knew you had a good head on your shoulders. Paul knew it, too. He also knew that if you ever needed him for anything, you would call. He was proud of you then, and if he were alive today, he'd still be proud of you," Tristan said.

Danielle looked straight ahead. "Even about this thing with Marc?"

Tristan didn't want to talk about Marc with her, but figured this time he would make an exception. He would tell her something she undoubtedly needed to hear. "Yes, *especially* about this thing with Marc. It wasn't your fault and Paul would be proud of how you're handling things."

He paused a moment and then said, "And stop thinking that perhaps you should have known what the guy was up to. There was no way you could have known, Dani, since he never gave you reason to suspect anything, especially something as outlandish as living a triple life. Marc was too smart and meticulous at what he was doing. He never planned to get caught and probably thought he never would. There's no telling how long things would have gone on without you or the others finding out. I don't wish death on anyone but he had to get caught eventually."

Danielle thought about Tristan's words, and then, deciding she would refuse to let Marc put a damper on her happy mood, she switched subjects and asked, "So, where are you taking me for lunch?"

He turned to face her when he stopped for traffic. "I've decided we can go back to the hotel and get room service."

When he saw her smile, he said, "I hope your smile means the plan meets with your approval."

She grinned. "Yes, it does."

He was tempted to ask why and decided not to bother. Hopefully she would *show* him why when they reached their hotel room. He was more than pleased with the way their relationship was progressing. Last night they had escalated things up a notch to become both lovers and friends. And their conversation in the department store, as well as the one they'd had a few moments ago, had proved they could talk to each other about practically anything. He had found the topic of quickies to have been rather interesting, as well as stimulating, to say the least.

"Will we stay in for dinner, too, Tris?"

"Let's play it by ear to see what we prefer doing later." He didn't want to tell her that by the time dinner rolled around she wouldn't have the strength to even get dressed.

Maybe it was his imagination, but he'd swear he felt the sexual tension between them thicken when he pulled into the hotel garage. When he pulled into a parking space, he glanced at her. She was staring at him. He'd have given just about anything to know what she was thinking. He definitely knew what was on his own mind.

"Ready to go up?" he asked evenly, not even wanting to think how he'd feel if she said no. He didn't have to think twice about what there was about her that made him want to make love to her every chance he got. All day, every day.

"Yes, I'm ready. Are you?"

He raised a brow, wondering if she was issuing a challenge. "Yes, I'm more than ready."

He saw her glance at his crotch. There was startling proof he could not hide. Deciding the sooner they got up to their suite the better off they'd both be, he unbuckled his seat belt and opened the car door, then came around to the other side to open hers.

He leaned over to unbuckle her seat belt and when his mouth was mere inches from hers, he swiped his tongue across her lips. He heard her swift intake of breath, then her startled groan.

"Sorry," he whispered against her moist lips. "I couldn't help myself." Then he straightened, took a step back and reached out his hand to assist her from the car.

Danielle felt the soles of her feet plant firmly on solid ground when she got out of the car. When she'd given Tristan her hand, the moment they'd touched she had felt it. The deep stirrings within her had intensified. For a woman who had gone without sex for eight months, she was definitely getting her fill now, making up for lost time.

"Come this way. It will be more convenient to use the elevator over there."

"All right."

They walked side by side, holding hands, and when they reached the elevator door, he moved to stand behind her. She could feel his aroused body pressed against her backside and she had to squeeze her eyes shut at the sensations that started flowing inside her. She shivered in response to them. Memories of what they'd shared last night and that morning, when he had kissed every inch of her body, filled hers, and the shivers increased.

He wrapped his arms around her waist, bringing her back even closer against him. "Are you okay?" He leaned forward to whisper the words beneath her earlobe. His breath bathed her neck in warmth.

She opened her eyes. "Yes, I'm fine. Why wouldn't I be?"

"You've gone quiet on me," he said.

"Um, I was just thinking about something." No need to tell him what that was. She thought about something else, too—her next conversation with Alex and Renée. When they asked how things were going with her and Tristan, what would she tell them? Would she admit they had crossed the line and were no longer just friends?

She remembered when she had seen Chris and Renée together at Alex and Hunter's wedding. Without even being told that something was going on between them, she had known. She had been able to pick up on how

Chris's gaze would follow Renée wherever she went, and the smiles they would exchange when they thought no one else was watching.

Danielle's mind was brought back to the present when the elevator door whooshed open and they moved aside to let a couple step out. Then Tristan took her hand and led her into the car. As soon as it began moving, Tristan's hand went to the panel box and pressed the stop button to suspend them between floors.

Danielle looked at him as if he'd lost his mind. "What are you doing?

Instead of answering, he turned and backed her against the wall. "Enjoying a quickie."

"What!"

And then she felt herself being lifted, along with her short skirt, as he wrapped her legs around his waist. Then his mouth was there, on hers, taking her tongue as if he had every right to it. She felt him work at his zipper, knew the exact moment he released his aroused shaft. And then his hands were between her legs, pushing aside her thong, and before she could blink, he was inside her. His first thrust hit her at an angle that sent shivers down her body. The second made her scream and the third made her come—right along with him. An orgasm struck their bodies at the same time and she tightened her legs around him to hold him in.

"Time to go, sweetheart," she whispered against his moist lips.

And while he stood her back on her feet and straightened her clothes before proceeding to straighten his, she still felt tremors touch her body, the aftereffects of her orgasm.

Before pushing the button to start the elevator up again, he glanced at her. She was leaning against the wall for support. He smiled as he said, "Now, sweetheart, you can't ever say you've never experienced a quickie. And just to put you on notice, there's a lot more where that came from."

Chapter 7

Tristan eased from Danielle's side when he heard his cell phone ring. He'd left it in the sitting area. Careful not to wake her, he moved toward the door, then paused for a second to look back over his shoulder at her.

His mouth formed into a smile. Danielle hadn't moved an inch, which was fine with him, and since she was barely covered by the sheets he could see the area between her thighs—the part of her body he enjoyed getting into the most. Her bare, firm breasts rose and fell evenly with her breathing while she slept.

Feeling deep stirrings in his body once again, he went out through the door and closed it behind him. He thought about what they had started on the elevator and what they had finished up here. Hell, on second thought, they really hadn't finished anything. When it came to this part of their relationship, nothing would ever be complete, especially when there were always new and exciting things to try.

He reached his cell phone and flipped it on. "Yes?"

"Tristan, this is Chris. How are things going?"

Tristan smiled. "Great. San Francisco is a beautiful city." Tristan knew Chris wouldn't be calling unless he had something he felt was important to share with him. "Did you find out anything else at Marc's apartment?"

"Yes, there's definitely a fourth woman. However, I'm still leaning toward her being a fiancée rather than a wife. I found a jeweler's receipt the other day and paid the jeweler a visit. It seems that Marc had a special wedding set exclusively designed. According to the jeweler, Marc had picked up the engagement ring almost eight months ago. The jeweler also indicated the engagement ring was six carats and cost close to half a million."

"Damn. Where did he get that kind of money?"

"My guess would be from a portion of that technology stock that rightfully belonged to Alex. I always figured he'd cashed in some of the shares."

Tristan shook his head. "Any idea the name of the woman who's walking around with a rock the size of Gibraltar on her hand?"

"No, but I'm determined to find out."

"And so is Dani. That woman's identity is the final piece for her. She needs to bring closure before she can move on."

"I understand, Tristan. More than anyone, I know the pain and misery my brother's deception caused and I owe it to Alex, Renée and Dani to bring closure. Now I feel I owe it to this fourth woman, as well. The jeweler didn't have her name, but he did mention that Marc told him he'd proposed to her at their favorite restaurant. I'm in Birmingham now with Renée, but I plan to fly back to Costa Woods and visit the restaurant to see if perhaps the owner remembers anything about Marc or the woman he was with. I'd like to have everything resolved before the wedding."

Tristan nodded. He hoped everything would be resolved by then, too.

Standing beside Danielle outside the door of Simon Craven's home, Tristan had to appreciate the beauty of the three-story structure. Majestically rising from a premium spot of land close to the Bay, the house actually left you breathless just from looking at it.

Craven, a very successful, highly paid fullback for the 49ers, had agreed to meet with them to discuss their interest in his family's business. Instead of meeting with them at the hotel, he had invited them to his home.

"Um, maybe I'm in the wrong business," Danielle said, interrupting Tristan's thoughts.

He smiled at her. He knew she'd earned a

nice salary as a model, yet had willingly walked away. "I'm fairly certain there're a number of guys who would just love to tackle you, whether it's out on the field or in the bedroom. Sorry, but I won't be giving them the chance, sweetheart."

At the moment Tristan didn't care one iota if he sounded possessive. Spending three days in a hotel room, eating, sleeping and making love with the same woman was bound to make you feel that way. Not that he was complaining, but they had only two days left in San Francisco and had yet to do any sightseeing. They'd had other, more pressing matters on their minds, a state of desperation they had needed to take care of. No question about it. Having an exclusive lover definitely had its merits.

His attention swung to the massive front door when it opened to a middle-aged woman in a maid's uniform. She smiled when she saw them. "May I help you?" she asked after giving them a cursory once-over.

"I'm Danielle Timmons and this is my

business partner, Tristan Adams. We're here to see Mr. Craven." Danielle returned the woman's smile. "I think he's expecting us."

"He is. I was asked to escort the two of you to the living room," she said, stepping aside for them to enter the massive foyer.

Danielle's gaze immediately went to the paintings on the wall, while Tristan's mind still whirled from how Danielle had introduced herself. Danielle Timmons. He knew she'd change her name back to her maiden name, but he wasn't aware until now that it was official. She was no longer a Foster—not that she ever legally was.

They followed the woman, and when they stepped into the living room, he couldn't help but appreciate the sheer elegance and luxury of Simon Craven's home. It was definitely a male domain, with furniture that showcased the buyer's exquisite taste.

"Mr. Craven will be with you in a minute," the maid said. "Please have a seat."

Danielle sat on the sofa and Tristan joined her. "Nice place, isn't it?" she asked him while glancing around the room. "And I love his taste in art."

Tristan had to admit he did, too. But what really captured his attention was the photo on the fireplace mantel of Craven on the back of a Harley. The bike was a beauty. Tristan did a quick trip down memory lane to the year before his grandmother Adams died. It was the Christmas she had surprised him with a motorcycle. He had turned seventeen the year before, and it was the last holiday the two of them spent together.

He could distinctively recall how the Timmons family had stuck by him and helped him make all the necessary funeral arrangements. His mother, Zora Adams's only child, had shown up a week after the funeral to inquire if anything had been left to her. When she discovered her only inheritance was the family Bible, she'd tossed it aside angrily and left town again. The last time Tristan had seen his mother was three years ago. She'd shown up, down on her luck, and asked for money.

Tristan turned when he heard footsteps on

the hardwood floor and glanced up to see Simon Craven enter the room. He noted the man's gaze swept past him directly to Danielle and stopped. Simon opened his mouth to speak, then seemed rendered speechless. Tristan wasn't surprised. Danielle had that sort of effect on men. And especially today wearing a blue, lace-trimmed Versace cami beneath a multicolored poplin shirt, a pair of skinny jeans and short, chocolate-colored suede boots on her feet.

Seeing the hulking NFL fullback so tongue-tied, Tristan thought it best to initiate introductions. But Danielle, being the effervescent and vivacious PR person that she was, stepped forward and extended her hand.

"Mr. Craven, I'm Danielle Timmons and this is my partner—"

"I know who you are, Ms. Timmons," Craven said, cutting in and taking the hand she offered. "I remember you well as a fashion model. We met once, years ago, at a party in New York."

The bright smile on Danielle's face turned

into an apologetic one. "Sorry, I don't remember. As a model I met so many people…."

The man finally released her hand, nodded and said, "That's understandable, but I do miss your face on magazines now."

Tristan thought it was time he introduced himself. Obviously Craven was taken with Danielle. "And I'm Tristan Adams, Danielle's business partner."

Maybe it was the way he had cut in to introduce himself, Tristan thought. Or maybe it was the look in his eye that said there was more to his and Danielle's relationship than business. Regardless of the reason, Tristan knew the exact moment Simon Craven picked up on it.

"Mr. Adams, I'm sorry about that," Craven said, giving him a smile that didn't quite reach his eyes. "I truly didn't mean to overlook you, but I was just taken aback when I walked in and saw Dani Timmons sitting in my living room."

"I understand. So we won't take up too much of your time, we would like to go ahead and discuss our interest in Shipping Source."

"Certainly, and I hope the two of you don't

mind that I've asked the company's attorney to attend so he can answer any questions you might have. I have very little dealings with my father's company."

"No, we don't mind," Tristan said, glancing at Danielle for affirmation. When she nodded in agreement, Tristan said to the man, "You have a beautiful home."

"Thank you." Craven looked at Danielle again before returning his gaze to Tristan. "And you, Mr. Adams, have a beautiful business partner."

"I think the meeting went well." Danielle threw her jacket across a chair when they returned to their hotel room. She tried brushing aside the thought that Tristan had been pretty quiet on the car ride from Simon Craven's home.

Tristan sat on the sofa and grabbed the remote. "Yes, things started going well once Craven and his attorney finally got down to business. I don't know which of them was worse. You'd think they'd never seen a beautiful woman before."

Danielle appreciated the compliment, but

couldn't ignore the irritation in Tristan's voice. "I thought they were just being nice."

He rolled his eyes. "Dani, Ray Stewart was coming on to you."

She ran her fingers through her hair in frustration. "No, he wasn't."

"Yes, he was."

Sighing deeply, she crossed the room and sat beside Tristan on the sofa. "Okay, and what if he was, Tristan? Why are you making such a big deal out of it?"

"I'm not."

She gave him an odd look. "Aren't you?"

Instead of giving her an answer, he stood and walked over to the window. *Was* he making a big deal out of it? He knew why it had bothered him when those two men had openly flirted with her. It was because he loved her.

But she didn't know that. She had enough on her plate without him overloading her with his emotions. Just because he was feeling them didn't mean he should expect her to feel them, too. In her eyes they were friends who were also bed partners.

"Tristan?"

He inhaled deeply as he turned to her. She looked as sexy as any one woman could look. Nothing detracted from her sexiness. Not even the frown on her face. It was a frown he'd put there.

He walked back over to her, took her hand and pulled her up and into his arms. "You're right. It's no big deal."

"No, it must have been a big deal to you," she said. "Those men flirted with me and it bothered you. Men have flirted with me before around you. Why is it bothering you now? Is it because we've slept together? Is that what's making you crazy?"

Crazy?

He wanted to laugh. He was in love with her, was acting like a besotted fool, and she thought he was acting crazy? Something snapped inside him. "I guess knowing that other men want you the way I have had you the last few days is making me crazy, Dani."

She shrugged out of his arms and moved toward her bedroom door. Before opening it, she paused and said, "Then I think you need to get over it."

She disappeared into the bedroom, closing the door behind her, and he could swear he heard it lock. He was tempted to check, but changed his mind. He was mad enough as it was.

He went into his own bedroom and all but slammed the door. Crap. He couldn't recall the last time a woman had gotten on his last nerve, had pissed him off to the point where he wanted to break something.

No, he hadn't liked the way those men had looked at Dani. He had seen lust in their eyes. When she had crossed the room to seek out the bathroom, they had watched her runway walk—straight and confident, hips swaying. It was a wonder Craven's and Stewart's eyes hadn't popped out of the sockets.

Tristan had just taken off his shirt to take a shower when he heard a knock on his bedroom door. Rolling his eyes to the ceiling, he crossed the room and snatched it open. Danielle was standing there, and from the expression on her face it was obvious she was still mad.

"Furthermore, Tristan," she said with hands on her hips, "I don't like it when you act jealous. There's no reason for it. It's not like we're real lovers or anything. We're just best friends."

He stared at her. *Real lovers?* He rested a shoulder against the doorjamb and crossed his legs at the ankles. "Please define 'real lovers' for me, Dani."

His question evidently caught her off guard, and he watched her frown deepen as she thought about how to answer him. Finally she said, "Real lovers are two people who are an item. They are…they are…"

He raised a brow. "They are what, Dani? Enemies? Then that would explain why we aren't a real couple, since we're friends. Or is it that they're strangers? That wouldn't work, either, because we *aren't* strangers. Or I guess you can say they're in love. But I guess you'll blow that away, too, since you think we aren't in love."

"We aren't!"

She had answered too quickly to suit him. "Okay, so we aren't in love," he said through clenched teeth. "Is that what makes us not a real couple?"

"Of course not. We're not a real couple because we're only doing this—"

"Doing what?" he butted in to ask.

She waved her hand through the air as if brushing away something. Like his nonsense. "Doing this. You know, sleeping together and all that stuff. We're only doing it because you needed it and I did, too. We were getting desperate. We're good together in bed. We're friends. But we don't own each other."

"Fine. You've made your point. Is there anything else, Dani?"

She shrugged. "No, I guess not."

"All right, then, if you don't mind I'm about to take a shower." He knew closing the door on her would be rude, but more than anything he wanted to be left alone and deal with his hurt. Each and every time they'd made love he'd thought of it as just that, making love. Apparently, though, she had seen it as nothing more than a case of satisfying needs.

"I'm going to order a movie on television later. Do you want to watch it with me?" she asked in a somewhat softer voice.

A part of him wanted to say yes, but another part—the one that was hurting—said, "No, I think I'll go over all those documents Stewart gave us to look at. If we're seriously thinking about taking on Shipping Source, then we need to know everything about the company, as well as its employees."

"All right, but if you change your mind, I'll be in my bedroom."

He watched as she turned and walked away, crossing the sitting room to her bedroom and closing the door behind her.

He ran a tired and frustrated hand down his face. Damn, it wasn't Danielle's fault that he loved her so much and that for the first time in his life he had wanted to hurt someone, a couple of people, over a woman.

He closed the door to his bedroom and began stripping off the rest of his clothes as he headed for the bathroom. He hoped the water blast from the shower would somehow wash some sense into him, because he suddenly felt like a love-smitten fool.

An angry Danielle snatched her cell phone off the dresser, wishing she could snatch the scalp off Tristan's head, instead. What on earth was the matter with him? With a soft curse she punched in a few numbers and waited. Boy, was she mad.

"Hello?"

"Alex? This is Danielle," she tried saying in a calm voice. "We need to talk. Hold on and let me get Renée on the line with us."

Before Alex could either agree or protest, she was placed on hold while Danielle switched over to punch in Renée's number. As soon as Renée answered, Danielle said, "Hold on Renée, let me pull in Alex." And with a flip of the wrist she had both women on the line with her.

"So what's going on?" she asked, determined not to let Tristan get on her last nerve, but inwardly acknowledging he already had.

Not surprisingly, it was Alex who answered. "I took Little Sweetie to be groomed today." And as if on queue, the sound of the dog's bark could be heard.

Danielle rolled her eyes. "That's nice. Have either of you heard anything more about—"

"Where's Tristan?" Renée interrupted to ask.

Danielle rolled her eyes again. "He's in his bedroom."

"Then why aren't you in there with him, instead of waking us up in the middle of the night?"

Danielle winced. She'd forgotten about the different time zones. "Sorry, guys, I didn't think to check. I'll let you—"

"What's wrong, Danielle? I can tell something is bothering you," Alex said in a soft voice. Danielle could hear genuine concern in her voice, and she knew that no matter what had brought the three of them together, somehow they'd become a sisterhood. Normally, when something bothered her she could go to Tristan and talk about it, but she couldn't do that in this situation because her problem *was* Tristan.

"He made me mad," she heard herself saying.

"What did he do?" Renée asked in a tone that indicated she was now alert.

"Well, we're thinking about expanding the business, so today we met with a potential business associate. The man and his attorney remembered me from my modeling days and they were very kind and—"

"In other words," Renée said, interrupting, "they fawned all over you, instead of paying attention to the business at hand."

Danielle rolled her eyes. "Like I said, they were nice and Tristan got mad about it."

"And why do you think he got mad, Danielle?"

"He evidently thinks that now that we've shared a bed he can—"

"Oh, the two of you finally got around to doing that, huh?" Alex asked sweetly.

Danielle frowned. "Look, Alex, I'm not in the mood."

"Then that's a personal problem. Hunter can attest that I'm always in the mood. He has no complaints."

"Alex, I think Danielle meant that she was not in the mood for us to make any comment about her and Tristan finally getting around to doing it." Renée's tone was the epitome of decorum, thanks to all those classes she'd told them she'd taken over the years.

"Oh."

Danielle shook her head. She couldn't help but smile. "You two are simply crazy."

"But you love us anyway, right?" Alex said, chuckling.

Danielle could imagine Alex wiping her curls away from her face when she'd made the statement. "Yeah, I love you guys." And she meant it.

"And Tristan loves you, Danielle," Renée said.

"Of course he loves me. I'm his best friend, although I could just kill him!"

"I think he's more than your best friend now, Danielle," Alex pointed out.

"No, we're still best friends, and that's what has me upset. He got mad at those guys for no reason."

"Sounds like there was a reason," Renée piped in. "He loves you. And I'm not talking about best-friend love or brotherly love. I'm talking about the same kind of love Hunter has for Alex and that Chris has for me. That man-love-woman kind of love."

"That's crazy!" Danielle said adamantly. "It's not that way between us."

"Then explain why the two of you slept together," Renée said.

When seconds passed and Danielle didn't say anything, it was Alex who spoke. "We're waiting to hear the reason, wife-in-law."

Danielle nervously gnawed on her bottom lip for a second and decided to come clean. "We were desperate."

There was silence on the other end. And then Alex asked, "Desperate for what?"

"For each other," Renée answered for Danielle. "Am I right, Danielle?"

Danielle nodded her head, and then when she realized they couldn't see her affirmation, she said, "Yes, you're right. Thanks to Marc, it had been a long time for me and I was in a bad way. And Tristan hadn't dated in a long time, either, and he was in a bad way, too, so we decided to use each other to take the edge off."

"And you think that's the reason the two of you slept together?" Renée asked in a soft voice.

"Yes, that's the reason." Danielle could imagine Renée, sitting in the middle of her bed, trying to keep her expression calm. Alex, she figured, was sitting up in bed patting Little Sweetie on the head. She thought of something. "Alex, where's Hunter?"

"He's lying beside me, asleep. I wore him out tonight."

Neither Danielle nor Renée had to ask how.

"Danielle, I think you need to take time to think about why Tristan got upset. There is a reason he got jealous, and until you come to terms with that reason, as well as the reason the two of you shared a bed, then he's going to always get mad when men come on to you."

"But we're nothing more than best friends," Danielle said, trying to get them to understand.

"Yes, you can still be best friends, but now the two of you are also lovers, and with that comes a load of responsibility and respect," Renée explained. "Tristan probably feels like those men disrespected him—not as your best friend, but as your lover. Think about it."

When Danielle didn't say anything, Alex asked, "Did the two of you use any kind of birth control?"

Danielle's shoulders stiffened. The corners of her lips twitched in a smile when she realized they hadn't. She couldn't help recall the comment Tristan had made that first night before they'd made love. He had made love knowing there was a possibility that each time he did so she could get pregnant. Yet it hadn't mattered, because he'd known she wanted a baby, had always wanted a baby, and he'd been willing to give her the one thing she'd always wanted. He'd taken it upon himself to right Marc's wrong.

"Danielle?"

She inhaled deeply. "No, we didn't use any kind of protection."

"Then you might want to add 'father of your child' to the list for Tristan," Alex said.

Danielle reached down and touched her stomach. "Yes," she said, wiping sudden tears from her eyes. "I might have to do that." She pulled in a deep breath. "Look, guys, I need some time by myself to think."

"That's a good idea. Call us back if you want to talk again," Renée said.

"I will and thanks. You two are special."

"We think you're special, too, being the oldest and all," Alex said with a grin in her voice.

A few moments later, after she'd hung up the phone, Danielle couldn't help but think that there'd been one good thing to come out of this mess with Marc. His three wives had become close friends.

And then she couldn't help but think of Tristan and their argument. They'd had arguments before but nothing as serious as this. This one had been heated and emotional. In her opinion he was acting crazy. But then, how was he supposed to act?

She didn't agree with Renée's and Alex's view of things—that Tristan was in love with her in a man-woman way. He'd always been overprotective of her, and now their sexual involvement only increased that protectiveness.

That was it. Tristan was her best friend. He was her lover, and like Renée and Alex had pointed out, he could also be the father of her child.

She felt a stirring in her stomach when she was reminded of the past couple of days and how much she'd enjoyed being with him— both in and out of bed. But she had to admit she really enjoyed the bed part. Sensual longing wrapped itself around her and she immediately recognized it for what it was: her body wanted Tristan. But more than anything, she wanted her best friend back.

Chapter 8

Tristan tossed the last of the documents aside, not able to concentrate any longer. The place was quiet, except for the hum of the television coming from Danielle's bedroom. Evidently she was watching the movie, one she'd invited him to watch with her. Instead, he'd turned her down to read a bunch of boring papers. At least they'd been boring tonight. Tomorrow they might hold his interest.

But not tonight.

Conflicting emotions washed through him.

Okay, he might have gotten carried away, might have gotten a little crazy, but he was a man. He'd seen the lust in those two men's eyes. If Dani had been a piece of chocolate, they would have gobbled her up. They hadn't even tried to hide their desire for her in a cloak of professionalism. Yet she thought they'd only been "nice." Granted, they hadn't made an outright pass at her or anything, but still…

The part she hadn't grasped yet was that she was his. He had plans for their future and the only involvement Craven or Stewart played in it was selling them the company they wanted to buy. The only good thing that had come from the meeting was that Craven had agreed to sell Shipping Source to them. Tristan would contact A&T's attorney tomorrow to draw up the necessary papers. After one final meeting, their dealings with Craven and his attorney would be over.

But then how would he handle things the next time a man showed interest in Dani? He'd never had to think about it before, but now he did. He had to give her credit for the way she'd handled herself with the two men, thanking them for their compliments but never leading them on in any way.

She had to know the degree of her attraction, he thought. She was stunningly beautiful and totally desirable. Men of all ages were easily drawn to her. That wasn't her fault and he hadn't wanted to make her feel that it was.

Dani didn't have a clue as to his true feelings. Because of that, in order to save his relationship with her, he would have to examine his actions carefully before taking any from now on.

A shiver went through him at the thought that because of their argument, he could have done irreparable damage to their relationship. He and Dani had argued before, but never about him being jealous of other men. He could only imagine what she was thinking about now.

Easing off the bed, he grabbed for his bathrobe. With no plans to leave his bedroom for the rest of the night, after his shower he'd pulled on pajama bottoms and nothing else.

He crossed the room and opened the

bedroom door to the common area at the same moment Danielle opened hers. Their gazes met, and immediately more love than he'd ever felt for any woman slithered through him, as potent as anything he'd ever experienced in all his thirty-four years.

Then another emotion gripped him. Sexual need. Looking so stunning, so incredibly sexy, she totally took his breath away. Like him, she was wearing a bathrobe, but hers was a plush short robe that showed a lot—a *whole* lot—of her legs. It wouldn't be much to keep a person warm on a cold night, but it was certainly doing a fine job of heating his blood.

It didn't take much to recall what was underneath that robe, how it looked, how it felt. He had touched it, tasted it, had gotten all into it and more times than not, hadn't wanted to get out of it.

He inhaled deeply, not knowing how to proceed. Her spine was straight, which probably meant she was still mad at him. Deciding to test the waters, regardless of whether he ended up sinking or swimming, he said, "I was just about to come looking for you."

He saw surprise light her eyes. "And I was just about to come looking for you, too," she said, taking a couple of steps toward him. Following her lead, he took a couple of steps toward her.

"I think we need to talk, Tris."

He nodded. "Yeah, I agree. Come on, let's sit on the sofa."

"All right."

He let her precede him and tried not to notice the sway of her hips when she walked. She sat on the sofa, and he thought he would play it safe and sit in the armchair across from her.

"Do you want anything from the bar?" he asked, leaning back in his seat. "Housekeeping left a note reminding us that it's fully stocked."

She shook her head. "No, I don't want anything, but you go ahead and get something if you like."

"No, I'm fine."

She nodded. "You said you were coming to look for me," she said, regarding him intently. "What did you want?"

* * *

The moment the question had left her lips, Danielle felt a multitude of sensations. It wasn't helping matters that his eyes were holding hers in a way she'd become familiar with, all but saying what he undoubtedly was thinking—he was much on the same wavelength as she was. Anger hadn't dampened the desire.

Over the past few days, whenever she'd asked what he wanted, his respond had been the same. *You, Dani. I want you.* And always the result had been her tumbling into his arms so he could take her. She wondered what his response would be this time.

He broke eye contact with her and glanced down at his hands. He had balled them into fists. He then looked up at her again. "I owe you an apology. You were right—I got kind of carried away about what happened at Craven's place. It wasn't your fault and I'm sorry if I came across like I thought it was."

She shook her head. "No, you didn't come across like that. It's just…all that jealousy confused me. You acted possessive and you've never acted that way before. But I thought about it and now I understand." She wouldn't tell him that she, Renée and Alex had actually discussed it in detail.

"And what do you understand?" he asked in a deep, husky tone of voice.

She shrugged. "I understand men get uptight about the women they sleep with, and although we're best friends I have to recognize the fact that we're also lovers, so you might see our relationship vastly differently from the way you saw it before, whereas I've been determined to keep it the same. I hadn't realized what sharing a bed with you entailed."

Slowly Tristan nodded. "Is that a good thing or a bad thing?" She shifted positions on the sofa and he saw enough of her bare thigh to make his stomach tighten. He took a deep breath.

"It's not really a good thing or a bad thing, Tris. It's a situation we have to deal with—unless you don't want to make love to me anymore."

The thought occurred to Tristan that he would rather cut off his arm than deny himself the pleasure of making love to her. "No, that's not what I want," he said, holding her gaze. "Is it what you want?"

She shook her head. "No, it's not what I want, either. I want to make love to you. I enjoy doing so immensely."

Desire flared in him, ripped at his most intimate parts. For him nothing was more exhilarating than being in her body, hearing her moan his name, feeling her grip him tight and milk him for everything he had, and then exploding inside her like he had every right to do so, over and over again.

"Do you enjoy making love to me?"

"If only you knew how much," he said softly. He took a deep breath that sounded ragged even to his own ears. "Making love to you is like heaven. And when I come inside you, I feel like a man on top of the world, a man totally fulfilled. For those precious moments you and I are the only two people on earth. Nothing else and no one else matters."

Tristan wasn't sure what possessed him to say all that. He had come one sentence shy of confessing his love for her. He wouldn't now, but one day he would. He promised himself.

Danielle rose to her feet and crossed the room to him. His senses were on alert with every step she took. She came to a stop in front of his armchair. Their gazes held for the longest time before she undid the sash at her waist and then eased the robe from her body, revealing one of the most daring and sexiest nighties he'd ever seen.

He swallowed tightly, reached out and skimmed his fingers along the hem of the brazenly short nightie that showed everything, especially the dark area between her legs.

"Show me, Tristan," she said in a voice that seemed to stroke the entire length of his arousal. "Show me how much you enjoy making love to me."

Tristan didn't have to be asked twice. He pulled her into his arms and kissed her like a man starving for her, and then he scooped her into his arms and carried her into her bedroom. He placed her on her feet while he removed her clothes and then his. Then he backed her up against the bed, with every intention of tumbling her onto it and following her there.

Danielle caught him unawares when she switched positions and pushed him down on the bed, instead, and quickly moved to straddle his body.

She smiled as she looked down at him. "First I think I want to show you how much I enjoy making love to you."

And then she lowered her mouth to his, swept her tongue inside his mouth and tangled with his tongue the same way he was known to do hers. Moments later she broke off the kiss and lowered her mouth to his chest, making slow, circular motions all over it with her tongue. She caught hold of a nipple and sucked it between her teeth, laving it while he repeated her name over and over, letting her know that what she was doing to him felt good.

As far as she was concerned, however, he hadn't felt anything yet.

Before she could give him a chance to react,

she shifted positions again and lowered her head to take him into her mouth. She felt his body jerk beneath her but held tight, not intending to go anywhere. She remained still while he absorbed the feel of being inside her hot, wet mouth. She knew the exact moment he did so, when he threaded his fingers through her hair.

And then she let her mouth begin pleasuring him, tasting him the same way he had tasted her. With a greediness she felt all the way to her toes, she ran her lips and tongue all along his aroused member and then took it back into her mouth again, giving it everything it rightly deserved.

Tristan called her name, heard the primal growl from his throat, but still, she refused to let up. He took the choice out of her hands—or out of her mouth—when he reached down and pulled her up before shifting positions and easing his hard shaft into her just seconds before he exploded.

The release triggered something within her and she screamed his name as a drowning orgasm hit her, as well. The last conscious thought that crossed her mind before she tumbled beneath the waves of ecstasy was that she could definitely get used to this.

Chapter 9

Danielle dabbed at her eyes thinking that Renée made such a beautiful bride. And she looked simply stunning, completely elegant in her white cocktail-length wedding dress embellished with delicate embroidery and pearl beading on the halter bodice. A classy pair of silver-and-white strappy sandals graced her feet, and the infamous diamond necklace—the one Marc had almost done away with—hung around her neck.

The bride and groom were now posing for

the camera. Renée had said they wanted lots of pictures to share with everyone. Danielle glanced around. It appeared that more than three hundred guests had been invited to the Sweet House. Built in the early 1900s, the building transported its guests back in time the moment they stepped inside its doors. The sheer elegance echoed a time long gone.

"You okay?"

Tristan didn't wait for an answer. He leaned down and wrapped his arms around her waist.

She looked at him. "Yes, I'm fine. Just happy. I don't know how to explain it, Tris, but it's like I've waited for this day to happen for Renée forever, when I've only known her for a little more than three months. How can that be?"

He smiled and pulled her closer into his arms, remembering the last two days they'd spent in San Francisco. They still hadn't gotten a lot of sightseeing in, but that was okay. What they *had* gotten in had been even more precious. Before, they'd known each other as best friends. Now they knew each other as lovers. He was more aware of her, more honed in to her wants and needs than ever before.

"The way I see it," he said, dipping his head to brush a kiss across her forehead, "is that something good came out of Marc's deceit, after all. He was able to make something happen."

She raised a brow. "What?"

"You, Renée and Alex. I don't know of three women who probably needed each other more."

She smiled at him before reverting her gaze to Renée and Chris. She then glanced over to where Alex and Hunter were standing. "I've thought that same thing lately. But still, there isn't closure for me."

He nodded, understanding. "It will come soon."

She stared at him. "Did Chris tell you something?"

"Yes. He was able to pick up a few leads on the woman's identity, but didn't have the time to follow up on anything. I thought we would fly home first, check on things, get the ball rolling for the purchase of Shipping Source and then fly to Costa Woods."

Gratitude shone in her eyes. "I know how busy we're going to be at A&T with the merger and all, but you'll take time off again for me?" she asked quietly.

He nodded as he took her hand in his. "Yes, I'll take time off for *us*. I won't be satisfied until we bring this thing to closure, as well."

What he wouldn't tell her was that only when there was closure would he share with her what he'd held inside him for so long. It was bursting to come out, but he had to be certain she would be ready not only to hear it, but accept it.

"Hey, guys," Alex said, as she and Hunter joined them. "How about all of us getting together for an after-the-honeymoon party on board the *Marc III* when the newlyweds return?"

"That sounds like a good plan to me," Tristan said, one arm around Danielle's shoulders now.

It sounded like a good plan to Danielle, too. She looked at Alex and saw the sly smile on her friend's face and knew what she was thinking. Even if Danielle hadn't shared with Alex and Renée the news that she and Tristan were lovers, it would have been quite obvious to everyone here that they were. He had always been a demonstrative person where she was concerned, but now he was even more so. And they'd been caught kissing—the tongue-deep-in-your-mouth-almost-down-your-throat kind—when Alex had stumbled upon them last night almost in this very spot after the rehearsal dinner. Alex had been out looking for Little Sweetie, who'd gotten away from her.

"Great," Hunter said, pulling his wife into his arms. "Then it's final. In three weeks the two of you, along with Renée and Chris, will join us in Atlanta."

The following two weeks were busy ones not only for Tristan and Danielle, but practically everyone at A&T. The first thing the partners did upon returning to the office was to call their top management together to advise them of what was in the works.

The main thing was to be sensitive to the people who had worked many years for Simon Craven's father at Shipping Source. Tristan and Danielle had given him their word that they would.

Shipping Source had more than forty offices spread out across the country, and Tristan and Danielle intended to make it their business to visit each one of them to assure the current employees that, starting out, few changes would be made. However, they both knew it was important to get many of their key players in place to ensure a smooth transition.

The purchase of Shipping Source went off without a hitch, and Tristan and Danielle were grateful for that. It had taken two weeks, instead of the one they'd counted on, but when it was over, they had celebrated with dinner and champagne. And that night, they continued the celebration in each other's arms.

"Tristan."

Danielle whispered his name from deep within her throat when a sexual explosion hit both of them at the same time. He held her tight while her legs locked around his taut and solid thighs, pulling him even further inside her.

This was what she looked forward to each

day, she thought. No matter how hectic things got at the office—and lately things had gotten crazier than ever—she knew she would always have this peace in his arms, after the turbulence of heated passion and earth-shattering ecstasy was shared.

Still locked in her body, Tristan pulled back far enough to look at her face. "I had your secretary clear your calendar for next week," he said in a deep, husky tone.

She lifted her lashes, just barely, to look at him. "We have another trip?"

"Yes," he said softly. "I talked to Chris today."

Her eyes widened in alertness. "Yes?"

"And he thinks he might have a positive ID on the woman."

Danielle's breath caught. They'd been too busy to talk about taking time away to follow up on Chris's last lead as they'd intended, and she'd been fine with that, had understood completely. Considering everything that was going on with the merger, there had been no way she could have asked Tristan to put everything aside to fly out with her to Costa Woods, so she hadn't. But neither had she forgotten that the loose end still existed.

"And?" she asked quietly.

"And Chris has told Renée and Hunter is telling Alex. He's asked me to tell you. Of course he's fully aware that you want to be the one to go and visit with the woman to tell her about Marc, assuming she doesn't already know."

Danielle nodded, knowing there was that possibility. "Did Chris tell you anything about her?"

Tristan shook his head. "He gave me a name and an address. He decided to leave it up to us how we handle things from here."

He paused a moment and then said, "There's something else I need to tell you. It's something Chris shared with me while you and I were in San Francisco. Because I didn't want to ruin your vacation, I made the decision not to tell you at the time, but I think before we make plans to go anywhere that it's something you should know."

"What?"

Tristan slowly disconnected their bodies and then eased off the bed. "Come on, let's take a shower first and then we'll talk."

Tristan walked into the kitchen and paused in the doorway. After their shower, which got delayed because he couldn't resist making love to Danielle again, he'd gotten a call from one of his new district managers in Savannah. The call lasted longer than he'd anticipated.

Danielle had come into the kitchen to make coffee. He couldn't help but admire what she was wearing, which was barely anything beneath another short robe. He smiled, thinking that since moving in, she had done wonders in gracing his kitchen each and every morning.

Although she claimed she hadn't officially moved in, she stayed with him every night. She'd put her house on the market and he knew she was working with a Realtor to find a condo close by the office. But he figured that was going to change soon enough, once he began doing whatever it took to make their relationship permanent.

"Coffee smells good," he said, walking into the kitchen and taking a seat at the table where she had placed a pair of mugs. She turned and smiled and reached for the coffeepot.

"Thanks. Is everything okay in Savannah?"

He nodded. "Yes. Reynolds wanted to make me aware of a huge shipment coming through. And he wanted us to know that the employees appreciated the new equipment."

"It was long overdue," Danielle said, pouring coffee into the mugs. "I'm glad Craven decided to go ahead and sell once he'd made the decision that he wanted no part of the business his father started."

Tristan couldn't agree with her more. The acquisition had been a blessing for everyone. Not only had A&T been able to retain Shipping Source's employees, most of whom had been with the company for years, they had posted a number of new positions at all the offices. The increase in hiring was a boost to the local economy where the offices were located.

Danielle sat down and glanced at him. He

saw the anxious look in her eyes. "So, what did you have to tell me about Marc?"

He could see that although she wanted to hear what he had to say, she was also uneasy about it. She had to put her coffee down when her hands began shaking.

He reached over and captured her hands in his. "Don't, sweetheart. It's nothing *that* serious."

"You mean Chris hasn't stumbled on a fifth woman?" she asked, affecting a playful tone.

"No."

"Okay, then, what is it?"

He leaned back in his chair. "When Chris was able to get back to Costa Woods earlier this month to do a more thorough job of going over Marc's apartment, he discovered a jeweler's receipt. He paid the jeweler a visit and found out Marc had an engagement ring exclusively designed for the woman."

Danielle raised a brow. "How exclusively designed?"

"To the tune of a half million."

"What!"

"Yes, I understand it was six carats."

Danielle shook her head. Tristan could tell she didn't want to believe it. "Where on earth did he get that kind of money?" she asked, stunned.

"Chris and I figured it was part of the loot that he embezzled from Alex's family's company." Tristan paused before adding, "The jeweler was also paid to design his wedding band and hers."

He knew Danielle was taking it all in before she asked, "Was the jeweler able to provide Chris with the woman's name?"

"No. But he was able to provide him with the name of the restaurant where Marc told the man he'd proposed to her. Because of his own wedding and then the honeymoon, Chris wasn't able to follow up on that until this week."

Danielle inhaled deeply. "And?"

"He visited the restaurant and the man remembered Marc. It seems Marc paid him a large amount of money for the restaurant to be closed that night at a certain time so that only he and his lady friend would be there."

Danielle blinked. She found it totally unbelievable that the man she·thought was her husband for five years and who'd stopped having a romantic bone in his body for the last three of them, had wined and dined this woman. "The restaurant's in Costa Woods?"

"No, it's in Dallas."

Danielle shook her head again. "Marc certainly got around a lot, didn't he."

"Apparently." After a few moments Tristan continued, "The restaurant owner remembered the woman, too. In fact, she patronizes his establishment on a frequent basis. And he's certain that's where she and Marc met, which was why he was so adamant about proposing there."

Silence stretched for a long moment before Danielle spoke. "Okay, just who is this paragon who deserved all of this lavish treatment?"

Tristan studied the contents of his coffee cup for the longest moment and then he looked at Danielle. "Her name is Catherine Hodges and she runs a school not far from the restaurant."

Danielle was staring at him as if she expected to hear more. He could tell she knew there was more. "Ms. Hodges runs a school for the deaf and blind," he added.

She raised a brow. "And?"

"She's blind, Danielle, and has been since birth."

Danielle paced the kitchen. She was livid. How could Marc stoop so low? Her heart went out to Catherine Hodges, and she couldn't help but wonder how badly the woman had gotten taken in.

"Dani, you're going to wear a hole in the floor."

She stopped and glanced at Tristan. They stared at each other for a long moment and then he stood with open arms and she wasted no time going into them. He held her tight, rubbed her back and whispered that things would be all right.

And then she cried.

He continued holding her, his arms enfolding her in his warm embrace, and she felt comforted in a way she never had before. And then she was scooped up in his arms and he carried her to the bedroom they were now sharing. When they got there, instead of placing her on the bed, he sat down and held her in his arms to let her continue to cry.

He rocked her and whispered that things would be okay and that in the end Catherine Hodges would be okay. Danielle wanted to believe that. She wanted to believe him. When she didn't have any more tears left to shed, Tristan placed her on the bed and undressed her before undressing himself. Then he pulled her into his arms again.

That was when Danielle realized just how much she loved him. How could she not love a man who handled her with such loving kindness? Such warm and tender care? She had fallen in love with Tristan Adams, her very best friend.

His hands moved all over her with both comfort and passion, and each stroke on her skin unleashed desire of a deeply potent kind. She felt her body tremble in anticipation, felt the area between her legs become heated with a need only Tristan could quench.

Then he lowered her to the mattress and joined her there. He bent his head and captured a nipple with his mouth. She felt his erection against her thigh. That was what she wanted. That was what she needed.

"Come inside me, Tristan. Now. Please."

She didn't have to ask twice. Immediately he moved over her and entered her in one hard thrust. *Yes!* This was what she needed, and her groans of pleasure were letting him know it, too.

He started moving then, thrusting into her with lightning speed and then slowing down as if to savor the moment. Over and over, in and out, deeper and deeper. She felt the welcome spasms start at the soles of her feet and work their way upward.

"Tristan!"

And then it came, just like she knew it would, and with a force that left her breathless, filled her with total completion and undiluted pleasure. She knew no matter what turmoil entered her life, she would always have this.

She suddenly felt tired, as if she couldn't hold her eyes open any longer, and she barely felt the hard jerking of Tristan's body when he got his own pleasure. But somewhere in the deep recesses of her mind, she heard him whisper, "I love you, Dani, with all my heart," just seconds before she drifted off to sleep.

Chapter 10

Danielle slowly opened her eyes to a new day, recalling every vivid detail about last night. But the thing that stood out most clearly in her mind was what Tristan had whispered to her when he thought she'd fallen asleep. *"I love you, Dani, with all my heart."* The words still echoed in her brain.

Alex and Renée had been right all along. Tristan did love her just as she knew she loved him. Even before he'd said the words, her heart had already made the decision.

Knowing he loved her in return made everything so complete.

She stretched and looked around, wondering where Tristan had gone. Then she remembered watching him hours ago through sleepy eyes as he eased out of bed before dawn, tugged on his running shorts before quietly slipping out of the room. It was Saturday and he usually went running then. Today was also the day of the company picnic. Their five hundred-plus employees and their families had been invited to the annual event, which was held each year the last Saturday in July. With the expansion of A&T, this year's picnic would be bigger than ever. A caterer had been hired to grill the ribs and chicken and prepare all the other tasty dishes they'd selected.

Danielle closed her eyes, feigning sleep, when she heard him return. Through lowered lashes she saw him glance at her before tugging off his shorts and heading toward the bathroom to take his shower.

The moment the door was closed she opened her eyes and slid out of bed. Moving quickly, she padded across the floor to the bathroom and quietly opened the door and eased in. She could barely see his body through the steamy glass door of the shower, but she could see in her mind's eye the broad chest and muscular shoulders, not to mention his taut, well-defined thighs. And what she considered the best-looking tush in all the world.

Her heart began to pound, a familiar sensation whenever she saw Tristan's naked body. This beautiful specimen of a man was not only her best friend and lover, but now the man she loved. That he actually loved her in return made her want to weep for joy. But she had done enough crying last night—and for all the wrong reasons. Marc and the pain he'd caused did not deserve another tear. Alex and Renée had been right. He had gotten his just deserts and it was time for each of them to move on and live.

Alex and Renée had done just that, falling in love and marrying men who would spend the rest of their lives making them happy. Deep down, Danielle knew she had found her soul mate, too. He was a man who had always been a part of her life, a man who was so attuned to her wants and her needs. A man who was her best friend.

The ceramic tile felt cool under her feet as she slowly strolled to the shower door. She eased it open and saw the surprise on his face. "Quickie time," she said, grinning.

He pulled her into his arms as the hot water washed over them both. Wasting no time, he lifted her off her feet and wrapped her legs around him, and just as quickly, he entered her. Her back pressed against the shower wall, he thrust into her. Once, twice. At the third thrust she was a goner, screaming his name while water poured all over them.

And then he was screaming hers and she felt the heat of his desire all the way to her toes.

After taking a shower they'd gotten back into bed and made love all over again. Now they lay cuddled in each other's arms, knowing they had to eventually get up and get moving, since the company picnic would start in a few hours. But Danielle knew there was something she had to ask him, something she had to know.

"Tristan?"

"Yes, sweetheart?"

"Last night, before I dozed off to sleep, you whispered something to me. You told me that you loved me with all your heart." She paused for a second and then rolled ahead and said, "Is that true? Do you really love me? And I don't mean the best-friend stuff. I mean the way a man truly loves a woman."

He had been stroking her back and at the start of her question his hands had gone still. Their eyes met and held for the longest time and then he began moving his hands again. "Yes, Dani. I love you. I didn't realize just how much until that day you called to let me know you wouldn't be coming in to work because you had eloped with Marc."

Her eyes widened. "You mean you've been in love with me all that time?"

A small smile touched his lips. "Yes, sweetheart, I've been in love with you all that time."

He didn't say anything more for a moment.

Then, "Does it bother you knowing that I love you?"

She shook her head. "No. Not unless it bothers you to know that I love you, too."

At his stunned look she smiled. "Here's love coming back at you, Tris, because I love you. I love you, Tristan Adams, with all my heart."

He pulled her into his arms and his mouth captured hers, and she knew at that moment that whatever happened from here on out would be okay because she was loved by a very special man.

She was loved and in love with her best friend.

"Strike two!"

Danielle turned and glared at Nero Long, their human resources manager who was acting as umpire for today's softball game. Nero had struck her out earlier so he was definitely not her hero today.

But neither was Tristan.

She glanced over to where he was supervising the three-legged races and saw Karin Stokes all but in his face and batting her false eyelashes at him. Danielle rolled her eyes. The woman, whether Tristan chose to believe it or not, was one hot mess. Danielle figured it was a good thing she and Tristan had confessed how they felt about each other; otherwise Karin would have continued coming on to Tristan and in a moment of desperation he might have actually relented.

"Strike three. You're out!"

Danielle lowered the bat and turned to glare at Nero. "And just how long will it be before you retire?"

The man laughed and he was doing it so hard his entire body shook—all two hundred-plus pounds of him. Knowing it would be a waste of time to challenge his call, she walked off the field and decided to go over to where Tristan was working hard to keep Hot Mess Karin at bay.

In a way Danielle felt he was getting what he deserved, since he hadn't taken her warning about Karin seriously until today. The woman had shown up at the company picnic wearing a short top and a pair of Daisy Dukes, and she had immediately sought out Tristan. She'd even had the gall to come up to her and ask where he was.

Because everyone who worked for the company was aware of her and Tristan's close friendship, Danielle figured none of them had a clue they were now an item, especially not Karin. The last thing she needed was for her and Tristan to become the main topic of conversation at the water cooler, but she figured something had to give. Now she knew how Tristan felt when he thought Craven and Stewart were showing a little too much interest in her.

"How are things going over here?" she asked, coming to join the group when the race was over.

Karin flashed her a smile. "Wonderful. I was trying to talk Tristan into partnering with me in the next race, but he's being difficult."

Danielle tried hiding her grin when she glanced at Tristan. He looked like he wanted to ring her neck. "I need to borrow him for a minute," she said, taking hold of his arm.

"Sure, just bring him back," Karin said, batting her false eyelashes again and smiling.

Danielle wasn't sure which of the two the woman enjoyed doing the most—flashing her smile or batting her eyelashes.

"I was wondering if you were ever going to come and rescue me," Tristan said, putting his arm around her shoulders.

"And not let you spend time with Hot Mess Karin? Are you kidding?" she asked.

"Hot Mess Karin?" Tristan burst into a laugh.

"I'm glad I'm able to amuse you. But on a serious note, sweetheart, you do something about her or I will. This is a company picnic where most of the employees bring their families, not a hot-pants contest."

Tristan glanced back over his shoulder at Karin. "Her shorts are kind of out there, aren't they."

"Out there, barely there. Yes, you could say that. And if you haven't noticed, a few of the wives are frowning since their husbands can't seem to keep their eyes off Karin. I've got a feeling a lot of them are going to be sleeping in guest rooms tonight."

Tristan sighed deeply. "I'll talk to her first thing on Monday. Oh, and by the way," he said, steering Danielle in the direction of the bleachers, "I've made all the arrangements. You and I are flying to Dallas on Wednesday."

"That soon?"

"Yes. Are you okay with it?" he asked.

"Yes. I'm okay with it."

Danielle had tried not thinking about Catherine Hodges and what situation she might find in Dallas. She had spoken to Alex and Renée, and both had given their support and suggested she handle the situation as she saw fit. The good thing was that the woman hadn't married Marc, at least.

Tristan took her hand in his. "You still want closure, don't you?"

She looked over at him. "Yes, I still want closure."

Closure.

That was the main thing on Danielle's mind when she and Tristan arrived in Dallas the following week. After checking into the hotel, they decided to wait until the following morning to show up at the school. They had called and Catherine Hodges's secretary made an appointment for them to meet with her.

"Do you think meeting her at the school is the wisest thing?" she asked Tristan that night after they were in bed.

"Not really," he said, pulling her into his arms. "But Chris didn't have her home address and phone number. When we arrive at the school tomorrow, let's play it by ear, since she doesn't know the reason we're meeting with her."

"All right."

That night after they had made love and Tristan had fallen asleep, Danielle cuddled beside him in his arms and smiled. She hadn't mentioned anything to Tristan, but her period was a couple of days late. She didn't want to get her hopes up, but the possibility she was pregnant filled her with more joy than she could ever imagine. If her period still hadn't shown up by the time they got to Atlanta, where they were to meet up with Alex and Hunter and Renée and Chris, then she would purchase one of those pregnancy test kits.

She drifted off to sleep hoping and praying that she was carrying Tristan's child.

"Ms. Hodges will see you now," the older woman said, smiling at them. "Please come with me."

Tristan took Danielle's hand in his as they followed the woman, who'd introduced herself as Sylvia Pinckney, Ms. Hodges's secretary. Upon entering the grounds of Land of Lakes School for the Deaf and Blind, they were impressed with what they saw. Students, some who couldn't hear and others who couldn't see, were participating in supervised sports of all types; other students were sitting in the classrooms using computers.

"How long has this school been in existence?" Tristan asked the secretary.

"For about three years now. It's a smaller institution than most around the country, but it serves its purpose. Ms. Hodges is doing an excellent job of running the place."

Danielle nodded. It was evident the school was well maintained. There were several separate classroom buildings on the property, as well as what appeared to be a gymnasium.

"We used to depend on donations," Ms. Pinckney was saying. "But even that sometimes was a struggle. We would have closed our doors for sure last year if it hadn't been for Mr. Foster."

Danielle almost missed her step and was thankful that Tristan had been holding her hand. "Mr. Foster?"

"Yes, Marc Foster. He was a huge supporter of the school before his untimely death."

Tristan and Danielle looked at each other before he said, "So you know that he's dead?"

The woman turned around and a sad smile touched her lips. "Yes. When he didn't show up at a very important function we knew something had to have happened to him, so we had Jules, one of our deaf students search the Internet. There was an announcement that he had passed away."

Ms. Pinckney's eyes widened just a little. "Did you know him?"

It was Danielle who responded. "Yes, we knew him."

Catherine Hodges was not at all what Danielle expected. An attractive woman, she couldn't have been more than twenty-six or twenty-seven. A friendly smile lit her face the moment she heard them enter her office.

Danielle glanced around the room and thought the setup was appropriate. Everything was within reach and all the books were in braille. When introductions were made, Ms. Pinckney mentioned that they'd known Marc.

Danielle watched how Catherine's face lit up. "Truly? He was a very special man who touched the lives of many of the students here."

"How so?" Danielle couldn't help but ask.

"In a number of ways. He's the one who got the computers for our classrooms and had the gymnasium built."

The woman paused. "You said your name was Danielle. Were you once Danielle Foster?"

Danielle's stomach tightened and she glanced quickly at Tristan. "Yes, I was at one time."

The woman's smile brightened. "Then I'm very happy to meet you. I'm sure Marc probably never mentioned me. He was always the secretive type when it came to his personal life."

Danielle forced a smile to her lips. "Yes, he was."

"He did tell me about all of you. He was proud of his sisters."

Danielle blinked. "His sisters?"

"Yes, you, Renée and Alexandra. He thought the world of you. He also thought a lot of his brother, Chris. I'm well aware that Marc and his siblings didn't share a close relationship. He talked about it sometimes and even admitted he had done some things to cause the rift. But now, with him gone, I hope all of you have forgiven whatever it was that kept the four of you from having a relationship with him. Believe me when I say that Marc was a remarkable man who gave me more than I could ever have given him. When it came to giving, he was one of the most unsel-fish men I know."

Danielle had to shake her head to make sure she was hearing right. All it took was the look on Tristan's face to know that she was. It was hard to believe that they were talking about the same Marc Foster.

"Are you here about the insurance money?" Catherine asked.

"The insurance money?" Danielle and Tristan said simultaneously.

"Yes. Marc had a number of insurance policies willed to the school, the total sum of which is enough to keep this school open and running for decades. When we learned of Marc's death, we had our attorney contact the insurance firm to collect the funds. Marc had given explicit instructions for us to handle things that way if anything were ever to happen to him."

"The two of you were engaged," Tristan said when he saw how speechless Danielle had become.

The woman glanced in his direction. "Yes, for a short while. He fancied himself in love with me and I loved him, too. In fact, I cared for him too much to let him sacrifice his life for me. We got engaged, but after a few weeks I came to my senses and broke off the engagement. That was about six months ago. I returned his ring, but he sold it and used the money to pay off the balance we had owing on the gym and to purchase some additional land the school needed."

When neither Tristan nor Danielle said anything, Catherine's smile brightened. "I've probably bored you to tears and you've yet to tell me why you're here."

There was a brief moment of silence, then it was Danielle who spoke in a soft voice. "Chris was going through Marc's things and found a receipt for the ring and traced it to here. I wanted to come and meet you, to finally get a chance to meet the one woman Marc undoubtedly loved."

Alex dabbed at her eyes. "I think you did the right thing, Danielle, by not telling Catherine

Hodges everything there was to know about Marc. It really wouldn't have served any purpose."

"I agree," Renée said, her eyes misty, as well. "I can't believe what Marc did for that school. For once in his life he was thinking about someone other than himself."

Danielle nodded. As soon as she and Tristan had set foot on the *Marc III*, she'd gotten Alex and Renée together for a short meeting, while Tristan told the guys what they'd discovered.

Renée reached out and took Danielle's hand. "Did handling things the way you did bring you closure, Danielle? Alex and I worry that you're still not going to move on with your life."

Danielle nodded. "Yes, it brought me closure. I am happy for Catherine Hodges, and I hate to say this, but I'm grateful that she met Marc and he was able to do so much for her and the school. I don't know what kind of relationship they had, but from the way she spoke about him, it was easy to see she cared a lot for him. She even admitted to being the one to break off the engagement because she felt Marc would make too much of a sacrifice to marry her."

After a brief pause it was Alex who asked, "So now that you've found closure, what will you do with your life?"

"Continue to love Tristan." At the looks of surprise on Alex's and Renée's faces, she smiled. "Yes, I've finally realized just how much I love him, and he has admitted to being in love with me. I hate to say it, but the two of you were right. There was more than friend-ship between me and Tristan, but I just couldn't see it. It took us spending time together, him being there for me when I needed him most, for me to realize just what a special man he is."

She glanced around before leaning in closer to them. "And I haven't told Tristan yet, since I just found out last night, but…I'm pregnant."

Both Alex and Renée let out whoops of joy. "Oh, Danielle, we are so happy for you!" Alex and Renée said simultaneously as they rushed from their seats to hug her.

"When will you tell Tristan?" Alex asked.

A huge smile covered Danielle's face. "Tonight. So don't either of you be surprised if we don't join you guys on deck for breakfast in the morning."

Later that night, after they'd taken a shower together and made love, Danielle was wrapped in the warmth of Tristan's arms. The night was perfect.

"What did Alex and Renée think about the way you handled things with Catherine Hodges?" Tristan asked her.

Danielle looked at him. "They agreed it was for the best. There was no need to tell Catherine our thoughts on the type of man Marc was, or to fill her in on all his bad deeds. The Marc Foster she knew and loved was a totally different man from the one we knew. He was unselfish and giving. I truly believe he loved her."

"So now have you found closure, Danielle?"

She shifted positions in the cabin bed and smiled at him. "Yes, but from all this I found so much more. I found a man who loves me and I love back."

She paused a moment and then said, "From the first, you were there with me, Tris, to hold my hand, wipe my tears and be by side. You let me know that no matter what I had to go through, I was never alone. I appreciate that. You have been so free in your giving, so unselfish in your love."

"I'll give you anything that's in my power to give, Dani," Tristan said softly, reaching out and touching her cheeks and noticing the wetness there. He cupped her face and brushed a kiss across her lips. "Why are you crying, sweetheart?"

She reached out and touched the hand he held to her face. "I'm crying because you, the man I love, my very best friend, will be wearing another title in about nine months. You will be the father of our baby."

Tristan went still. He stared deep into her eyes and then a smile touched his lips. "Are you saying that you're pregnant?"

Danielle laughed. "Yes, father-to-be. That's

exactly what I'm saying. You made my dream come true, Tris. You gave me the one thing that I wanted in life. I love you."

"And I love you," he said, pulling her into his arms and holding her tight. "And now I'm asking you to give me yet another title, one that I will wear just as proudly as the others. Your husband."

He pulled back and gazed into her face. "Will you marry me, Danielle? Will you spend the rest of your life with me?"

Danielle smiled as tears glistened in her eyes. "Yes! I would be honored to be the one you call wife."

She leaned forward and wrapped her arms around his neck and kissed him, putting everything she felt and more into that kiss, knowing this was the start of the rest of their lives together.

Epilogue

Alex and Renée shared tears of happiness as they watched Danielle and Tristan exchange their wedding vows. It was a beautiful September day in Port St. Lucie, and it seemed the entire town was present at the Forest Grove Baptist Church for the occasion.

"I just knew it would end this way for all three of us," Alex said happily. "I just knew it."

Renée glanced over at her. "And how did you know?"

"Because I felt it. Marc's dying was not in vain. I may have lost a husband—or someone I thought was my husband—but I gained a lot more in return. I got you and Danielle for life."

Renée laughed. "Yes, for life."

Their attention was pulled back to the wedding when a cheer went up. The pastor had just pronounced Tristan and Danielle husband and wife.

A few minutes later, after Tristan picked up his bride to carry her out of the church, Alex and Renée were joined by their husbands.

"We tried to tell Danielle that Tristan was in love with her," Alex said matter-of-factly. "But she refused to believe us."

Renée smiled. "It just wasn't time for her to believe us, Alex." She glanced at her husband. "A woman will eventually know when she is in love and is loved."

Alex smiled and looked at Hunter, feeling the very essence of Renée's words when she looked into her husband's eyes.

"Now that the three of you are married," Chris said, "what's next?"

Both Alex and Renée leaned up and whispered to their husbands at the same time. "Babies."

It took Hunter and Chris a minute to realize that announcements had just been made. Overjoyed, they swept the women they loved into their arms.

Later that night as they spent their honeymoon on the cruise ship they had boarded a few hours after their wedding, Tristan pulled his wife, the mother of his child, into his arms. Come spring, he and Danielle would have a little one to love. They had decided if it was a boy, they would name him Paul, and if it was a girl, she would be called Paulette.

"I love you, sweetheart," he whispered to her.

"And I love you back."

She did and she would make sure that for the rest of his life he would know it.

She thought about how beautiful their day had been, how wonderfully everything had gone, and knew she wouldn't have done anything differently. Alex had offered the use of the *Marc III* for the wedding, but Danielle knew there was no way she would cheat all the good people of Port St. Lucie of being witness to an Adams and Timmons match-up.

Besides, a lot of her modeling friends had come, and she'd been elevated to celebrity status all over again.

"What are you thinking about, sweetheart?" Tristan asked.

"About how happy I am." She looked at him. "And are you happy?"

He chuckled. "If I was any happier I'd probably burst at the seams."

"Well, I guess now is a good time to tell you, since I'm sure Hunter and Chris know by now."

Tristan lifted a brow. "Know what?"

"Come spring, they will become fathers, too."

The smile that covered Tristan's face was priceless. "No kidding?"

"No kidding. So I'm sure the three of you will have a lot of stories to swap this time next year."

"Yeah, and I'm looking forward to it."

"So am I, Mr. Adams. So am I."

And then she pulled his mouth down to hers for another kiss. Just one of many they would share over their lifetime.

* * * * *

We hope you enjoyed JUST DESERTS.
Following is an excerpt from Brenda
Jackson's next Kimani Romance novel,
THE OBJECT OF HIS PROTECTION.
Look for it in November 2008.
It is part of an exciting new series…

THE BRADDOCKS: SECRET SON
POWER, PASSION AND POLITICS
ARE ALL IN THE FAMILY.

Three sons and a daughter take up the
mantle after the death of a powerful Houston
patriarch, and along the way each sibling
will find an enduring love to last a lifetime.

HER LOVER'S LEGACY by Adrianne Byrd
August 2008
SEX AND THE SINGLE BRADDOCK
by Robyn Amos
September 2008
SECOND CHANCE by A.C. Arthur
October 2008
THE OBJECT OF HIS PROTECTION
by Brenda Jackson
November 2008

Chapter 1

"I might as well come in, since it doesn't appear that you're busy."

Charlene Anderson didn't need to look up to know who the deep, husky voice belonged to.

Drey St. John.

She did, however, glance over at the small heart-shaped ceramic clock sitting on her desk, the only part of her work area that wasn't buried deep in paperwork. Drey was early, although his visit wasn't unexpected. He was a private investigator and she was a forensic scientist in the coroner's office. It wasn't unusual for him to drop by occasionally to harass her for forensic information that would help with his investigation of whatever case he was involved with.

"If you think I'm not busy, look again," she said, not taking her eyes off the document she was reading. "Now, get lost."

She knew he wouldn't go away. He never did. That didn't bother her, since she had a weak spot for the rebel private investigator and actually looked forward to seeing him, although she would never admit such a thing to him. His visits were the only high point in her rather dull life. At twenty-seven, she made work her focus, and no matter how you looked at it, dead bodies didn't equate to great dates. Her social life was practically nonexistent and, of all things, she was still a virgin.

While attending Oklahoma State University, she had been too busy making the grades to get involved with anyone and had figured things would change once she finished school and got her career off the ground. Since she looked decent enough, she had been convinced that she would eventually meet some nice guy and get serious. That never happened. For her it always seemed to be all work and no play.

"Don't you ever get tired of messing around with the dead?"

It was then that she glanced up. Drey was drop-dead gorgeous, definitely a living, breathing specimen of a sexy male—tall, dark and ultrahandsome. There was no doubt about the fact that at thirty-three he was very good-looking.

He had skin the color of creamy rich chocolate, dark hair and slanted dark eyes. All she knew about him was the tidbit she'd overhead from a group of women discussing him one day at lunch. According to them, his mother was half-Chinese. If that was the case, she had passed a strikingly exotic look on to her son. Charlene had also heard that his middle name, *Longwei,* meant "dragon strength" in Chinese. It was her opinion that it suited him because of his well-defined muscular physique.

"Not really," she finally said, taking her eyes off him and making an attempt to return her focus to the document in front of her. "At least I don't have to worry about the dead giving me a hard time."

"Yeah, I imagine they wouldn't."

She didn't have to glance up to know he was no longer standing in the doorway but had come into her office. Her heart began beating twice as fast. The man had a way of getting to her. In addition to her erratic heartbeat, there was this unexplainable fusion of heat that always overtook her whenever he was near, not to mention the way the air surrounding them always appeared to be charged. It was apparent that she was the only one who picked up on such vibes—she seriously doubted he noticed, since he was usually busy trying to pump information out of her.

When he halted before her desk, blocking her sunlight, she decided to glance up, but took a deep breath before doing so. "And what got you out of bed so early this morning?" she asked, and immediately wished she hadn't when a vision of him getting out of bed—almost half naked—filtered through her mind. It was a nice vision, but dangerous ground for her mind to be on.

"I need your help with something."

She rolled her eyes. "What else is new?"

"You're the best there is," he said, smiling. And she wished he wouldn't do that. He was sexy enough without the killer-watt smile.

"Flattery will get you nowhere, Drey."

"What about dinner tonight?"

She placed her pen down and leaned back in her chair. "This must be some case if you're willing to spring for dinner."

She watched the emotions that crossed his face, emotions he rarely let show. He was angry and upset, but was holding it in. Something about the case he was working on was bothering him. She could feel it.

"It is," he finally said. "And the answers may very well come from a stiff brought here last week by the name of Joe Dennis."

Charlene turned toward her computer and typed in the name. "Nothing has been done with him yet. He's on Nate's list to do later today." Nathaniel Thurmond was her boss. "What exactly do you need to know?"

His tensed features relaxed somewhat when he said, "Anything you can tell me."

She nodded. He understood there were limitations as to what she could share and she appreciated the fact that he had never asked her to cross the line in doing anything unethical. Not that she would. "In other words, anything out of the ordinary."

"Yes."

"Okay. I'll take a look at the report when Nate's finished. As you know, my boss is very thorough." She cleared her computer screen and turned back to him. "I'll let you know if I notice anything."

"Thanks, and I'm serious about dinner."

"But I'm not." It hadn't been the first time he had hinted at the two of them going somewhere to grab something to eat. She could barely handle her reaction to him now; she didn't want to think how things would be if she had to share a meal with him. Besides, she considered him business and she didn't mix business with pleasure. "Maybe some other time, Drey," she said, knowing it wouldn't happen.

"You said that before."

Not that she was foolish enough to think that it mattered to him. "And I'm saying it again. I'll call you if I learn anything."

"Thanks, Charlie. I would appreciate it."

Charlene glared at him, something she did whenever he called her that. "Do I look like a Charlie to you?"

He smiled. "Hard to say with that lab jacket, since that's all I've ever seen you wear."

Before she could give him a blazing retort, he turned and left.

The smile remained on Drey's lips as he got into his car. For some reason he enjoyed getting a rise out of Charlene. In fact, the thought of seeing her today had pretty much kept his anger at bay, although it was creeping back on him now. He was discovering that being lied to all his life was something he was having a hard time dealing with.

Before starting the engine, he sat still for a moment and stared out the window, thinking about the conversation he'd had with his mother, Daiyu Longwei, a few days ago. She had practically shattered his world when she had told him that Ronald St. John, the man Drey had assumed for the past thirty-three years was his father, was not. Instead the man Drey had considered his mentor, Congressman Harmon Braddock, was actually his biological father.

The hands that clutched the steering wheel tightened as his mother's words flowed through his mind. *Ronald St. John was not your biological father. Harmon Braddock was.*

Sighing deeply, Drey started the engine thinking that, in essence, he was investigating his own father's death. His own father's *murder,* he immediately corrected, since he was convinced Harmon Braddock's car accident was deliberate. Someone wanted him dead and Drey was determined to find out why.

Something else he couldn't put out of his mind was that the very people who had hired him to find out the truth were Harmon

Braddock's offspring—and his siblings. He shook his head, knowing they didn't have a clue as to what his relationship to them was. At some point he would have to tell them, but not now. He wasn't ready to go there yet. It was bad enough that he had to deal with it. Besides, how his own mother played into the investigation was still a mystery, since it was well documented that less than an hour before his death, Harmon had tried contacting Daiyu. Hell, he hadn't known the two even knew each other, and none of the Braddocks knew that Daiyu was his mother. He didn't like withholding information of any kind from clients, yet that was exactly what he was doing.

He had known the congressman for a number of years, and mentally recalled everything he knew about him. When Ronald St. John, the man Drey had adored as a father, was killed in the line of duty as a police officer when Drey was fifteen, he had taken it hard, since the two of them had always been close.

It was during that time that Congressman

Braddock took an interest in him. And later in life when Drey had felt himself getting tired of his own career as a police officer, it had been the congressman who had encouraged him to start his own private investigating firm and had gone so far as to keep him on retainer during those times he'd been trying to make ends meet. He would be the first to admit that over the years, Harmon had become the father figure that he'd lost.

To be quite honest, when he'd first heard of Harmon's car accident he'd had no reason to suspect foul play, even when the other Braddocks had. But now Joe Dennis's death was raising his suspicions.

Drey brought the car to a stop at the next traffic light as he replayed the facts of the case over and over in his mind as he knew them. Congressman Braddock had been killed in a car accident. The skid marks on the road had been consistent with a car losing control. It seemed Harmon was heading for the airport—which was another mystery, since Gloria Kinsley, the congressman's executive assistant, who'd known Harmon's every move, hadn't known about any planned trip.

Another thing that baffled everyone was why the congressman was driving when his personal driver, Joe Dennis, usually was the one to drive Harmon everywhere he went.

And now Joe was dead, and according to the police report there didn't appear to be a robbery. There was no forced entry and nothing seemed out of place. Someone just wanted Joe dead. Why? And exactly what had been the cause of death?

Drey had a lot of unanswered questions, but at least the latter he felt fairly confident would get answered soon enough, once he heard from Charlene. With that certainty, his thoughts couldn't help but go back to the efficient forensic scientist. They might bicker back and forth every chance they got, but they understood each other. She was as dedicated to her profession as he was to his.

In the two years he'd known her, he'd never met another no-nonsense woman quite like her and he found her to be sharp, intelligent…and definitely beautiful. The last he tried not to dwell on too much. Seeing her in that lab coat all the time should have been a turn-off, but instead it was a total turn-on because he often wondered just how she looked beneath it.

But what he liked about her most of all was that she didn't hesitate to give him hell if she thought he deserved it, and that made their verbal sparring that much more fun.

And for some reason he had felt the need to see her this morning. Of course, there had been that matter regarding Joe Dennis, but it seemed once his mother had hit him with the news of his parentage, he needed the light-hearted banter he and Charlene enjoyed to take his mind off things.

Lately, all his relationships with women had been casual, just the way he wanted. He didn't have time for any type of serious indulgence and the last thing he needed was someone getting too clingy. He could tell that Charlene wasn't the clingy type. Besides that, their relationship was strictly professional. He had asked her out to dinner a few times, after the information she had given him had helped him solve a case. But she had refused, and he hadn't had a reason to push.

Frowning, he turned the corner onto the road that would take him to his office. Later he would drop by headquarters to recheck the police report on Joe Dennis's death, to see if there was anything that had been missed. Drey was determined to find out everything he could.

"I'm leaving to attend a meeting, Charlene. Don't stay too late."

She smiled as she glanced over at Nate as he slipped into his jacket. "I won't. In fact, I intend to leave on time today."

When he tried smothering a cough, she said, "And please take my advice and do something for your cold. You're passing germs, and I can't afford to get sick."

Nate's chuckle was the only sound he made before leaving the room. She stretched her legs, trying to recall just how long the two of them had worked together. Three years. He was an easy enough boss, although he could be demanding at times. The city had this thing about doing more with less, and amidst a number of budget cuts the coroner's office was operating on slim funds, which could barely keep up with the number of suicides and suspicious deaths they handled each year. The only saving grace was that Nate left her alone to do her job, not to mention that the nice salary increases she'd gotten each year let her know her hard work and dedication hadn't gone unnoticed.

Nate was middle-aged at forty-four, and as far she knew, happily married after over twenty years. He had a son and daughter who were both in college, and his wife, Joanne, was a pediatrician in the city and a very likable person. From the conversations Charlene and Nated share she knew he adored his wife.

She glanced at the clock and saw it was almost five in the afternoon. She stood and stretched after logging off her computer. She then recalled Drey's visit and what he had asked her to do. Deciding now would be the best time since Nate had left for a meeting, she went into the autopsy room to take a look at Joe Dennis's chart. Nate had just finished performing the autopsy on Dennis and the chart was still lying on the table. She picked it up and began to read.

Trauma to the head, consistent with an attack from behind, was noted, as well as several other bruises to the man's neck and shoulders. She raised her brow at the indication that a key had been removed from the victim's stomach. She glanced over at the key that was on the table. Why would anyone swallow a key?

Deciding that was definitely something worth mentioning to Drey, she left the autopsy room, determined to call Drey once she got home. She was about to exit the room when she heard Nate talking loudly to another man. That struck her as odd, because in all the years she had worked with Nate, she had never known him to raise his voice. And why had he returned in the first place? Most of the time his meetings lasted an hour or longer.

Concluding the conversation was none of

her business and the best thing to do was to leave before Nat found a task for her to do, she headed for the door and couldn't help noticing that the voices had gotten louder. She paused. Nate was definitely upset about something, but so was the man he was talking to. His voice was deep and sounded slightly hoarse. She could only assume, since she hadn't been sitting at her desk when Nate returned, that he thought she had left for the day. Not wanting to eavesdrop on Nate's argument any longer, she slipped out the door.

Drey heard his cell phone ring the moment he stepped out of the shower. Wrapping a towel around his waist, he quickly walked out of the bathroom to pick it up off the nightstand next to his bed. "Yes?"

"Drey, this is Charlene."

He felt a churn in his stomach and immediately thought, not for the first time, that she had such a sexy phone voice. There was just something about it that made goose bumps form on his skin. "Charlie," he said, not liking the boost to his testosterone and deciding by calling her that it would keep things in perspective.

She paused a moment, and he figured she'd done so to blow off a little steam, before saying. "I was able to take a look at Nate's report on Dennis."

The way she said the statement alerted him there was more. "And?"

"And I noticed a couple of things I figure you might want to know."

"Such as?"

"There was trauma to the head, which is consistent with some sort of an attack from behind."

Drey nodded. Not that the police had been much help. He had paid a visit to the headquarters after lunch, hoping to learn something not already on paper, but he hadn't. For some reason it seemed everyone had closed lips. Usually they would become loose for a former member of their own, but today this was not the case. And unfortunately, Detective Levander Sessions, his former partner while on the force, was out of town. Like Charlene, he could always count on Sessions to tell him what he needed to know.

"And there's something else pretty strange about Joe Dennis."

Charlene's statement cut deep into his thoughts. "What?"

"He swallowed a key."

"Excuse me?" Drew said, certain he hadn't heard her right.

"I said he swallowed a key. One was taken out of his stomach."

Drey rubbed his chin thoughtfully. "Are you sure?" Immediately he knew he had made a mistake in asking her that. In all his dealings with Charlene, he had come to realize that she was a professional who knew her business.

"Of course I'm sure. Not only did I read it in the report, but I saw it myself. Nate hadn't removed it from the table."

Drey didn't say anything for a moment while his thoughts were turning. Had Dennis swallowed the key to keep it from getting into someone else's hands? Was the key a link to Harmon's death? Those were questions he intended to get answered. "What sort of key was it?" he asked.

"I think it was too small to be a door key. It was more like the size of a locker key or safe deposit box key."

He rubbed his chin again, his curiosity igniting. "I need a copy of that key," he said, placing the phone on speaker so he could get dressed.

"That's not possible, Drey. I don't mind passing information on to you if I think it will help your case, but I draw the line at removing anything that could later become evidence from the premises."

"And I'm not asking you to," he said quickly.

"Well, what are you asking me to do?"

He could hear the agitation in her voice. The last thing he wanted to do was get her teed off, especially now since he needed to find out everything he could about that key. "I'm asking that you provide me with a mold of it in wax—you use a small kit that resembles a lady's compact."

She didn't say anything for a moment, as if contemplating his request. And then she asked,

"But what good is that when you don't know what the key goes to?"

"I'm determined to find out. So will you get an indentation of that key?"

"I don't know, Drey…"

"Please." If he sounded desperate, there was no help for it. He needed to know everything about Joe Dennis's death, and now that he knew it hadn't been from natural causes, he was more determined than ever to find out what had happened.

He could hear her deep sigh and felt his heart begin to beat wildly in his chest. Even her sigh was a turn-on. "Okay, fine," he heard her say. "Where am I supposed to get such a kit?"

"I have one."

"How convenient."

He couldn't help but smile. If he solved the case and was able to link it back to Harmon's death, then he owed her more than just dinner. "Meet me somewhere tonight so I can give it to you."

"Where?"

"You name the place. Better yet, if you

give me your home address I can drop it off there."

He heard her hesitation and was about to throw out another option when she said, "That's fine, since I really don't want to go back out tonight. I live in the Rippling Shores Condos."

He knew the area. It was a newly developed subdivision of really nice townhomes. "I know where it's located. What's the condo number?"

She rattled it off to him and he saved it in his memory. "I'll be there in less than an hour."

He smiled when without even a goodbye, she hung up the phone on him. For some reason he was looking forward to seeing her without her lab coat.

Dark, rich and delicious…how could she resist?

NATIONAL BESTSELLING AUTHOR

ROCHELLE ALERS

The Sweetest Temptation

Book #2 of The Whitfield Brides trilogy

Faith Whitfield's been too busy satisfying the sweet tooth of others
to lament her own love life. But when Ethan McMillan comes
to her rescue, he finds himself falling for the luscious pastry
chef…and soon their passions heat to the boiling point!

Meet the Whitfields of New York—experts at
coordinating other people's weddings, but not so great
at arranging their own love lives.

Available the first week of July wherever books are sold.

ARABESQUE®

www.kimanipress.com

KPRA1020708

Bound by duty...or desire?

forget me not

NATIONAL BESTSELLING AUTHOR

ADRIANNE byrd

Detective Jaclyn Mason's investigation of her partner's murder plunges her into a world of police corruption—so she seeks help from her partner's best friend, FBI agent Brad Williams. Brad ignites passion beyond Jaclyn's wildest dreams...but can he overcome her fragile trust to convince her that it's true love?

"Byrd proves once again that she's a wonderful storyteller."—*Romantic Times BOOKreviews*

Available the first week of July wherever books are sold.

ARABESQUE®

www.kimanipress.com

KPAB1050708

GUARDING HIS
BODY

…as if it was her own!

Bestselling author
A.C. ARTHUR

Renny Bennett's new bodyguard just might be more
dangerous than any threat to his life. Petite Sabrina Dedune
has a feisty, take-no-prisoners attitude…and an irresistible
allure that's to die for. But after one searing kiss,
Renny's is not the only heart at risk.

TOP SECRET
ROMANCE ON THE RUN

Coming the first week of July wherever books are sold.

KIMANI™
ROMANCE

KPACA0730708

Welcome to the Black Stockings Society—
the invitation-only club for women determined
to turn their love lives around!

Power Play

Book #1 in a new miniseries
National bestselling author

DARA GIRARD

When mousy Mary Reyland discovers her inner vixen,
Edmund Davis isn't sure how to handle the challenge. Edmund
enjoys being in charge, but the new sultry, confident Mary
won't settle for less than she deserves, in business or pleasure....

Four women. One club.
And a secret that will make their
fantasies come true...

Coming the first week of July wherever books are sold.

KPDG0740708

The laws of attraction…

PROTECT
and SERVE

Favorite author

Gwyneth Bolton

Detective Jason Hightower has waited fifteen years to find
out why Penny Keys left him. Penny hasn't returned home
to face her difficult past…or the man she still loves.
But Jason wants answers, and this time nothing
will keep him from the truth.

HIGHTOWER HONORS

FOUR BROTHERS ON A MISSION TO PROTECT, SERVE AND LOVE.

Coming the first week of July wherever books are sold.

KIMANI
ROMANCE

www.kimanipress.com

KPGB07507Q